From a mother as she grapples with age, infertility and an increasingly distant husband to a former children's television star who tries to rebuild his life after being hospitalized for 'exhaustion'. From an elderly woman mourning the loss of her husband to a single mother who finds the strength to protect her flamboyant six-year-old son, these stories follow the hazardous terrain of everyday life, revealing the deceptions, heartbreak, and vulnerability familiar to us all. *When It Happens to You* is an unflinching yet poignant examination of the intricacies of the human heart and an auspicious literary debut.

'Molly Ringwald understands how families work and uses her considerable talents to make them come alive on the page'
Gary Shteyngart, author of *Super Sad True Love Story*

'These stories sizzle with rare insight about the reverberations of betrayal and of love . . . an impressive fiction debut'
Robin Black, author of *If I Loved You, I Would Tell You This*

WHEN IT HAPPENS TO YOU

ALSO BY MOLLY RINGWALD

Getting the Pretty Back

A NOVEL IN STORIES

WHEN IT HAPPENS TO YOU

MOLLY RINGWALD

**SIMON &
SCHUSTER**

London · New York · Sydney · Toronto · New Delhi

A CBS COMPANY

First published in Great Britain by Simon & Schuster UK Ltd, 2012
A CBS COMPANY

1 3 5 7 9 10 8 6 4 2

Simon & Schuster UK Ltd
1st Floor
222 Gray's Inn Road
London WC1X 8HB

www.simonandschuster.co.uk

Simon & Schuster Australia, Sydney
Simon & Schuster India, New Delhi

A CIP catalogue record for this book is available from the British Library

HB ISBN: 978-1-47111-348-2
TPB ISBN: 978-1-47111-423-6
EBOOK ISBN: 978-1-47111-350-5

Designed by Lorie Pagnozzi
Printed and bound by CPI Group (UK) Ltd, Croydon, CR0 4YY

FOR PANIO

A pity. We were such a good

And loving invention.

An aeroplane made from a man and wife.

Wings and everything.

We hovered a little above the earth.

We even flew a little.

YEHUDA AMICHAI

But the disparaging of those we love always alienates us

from them to some extent. We must not touch our idols;

the gilt comes off in our hands.

GUSTAVE FLAUBERT

CONTENTS

WHEN IT HAPPENS TO YOU

THE HARVEST MOON

AS FAR AS GRETA KNEW, there was nothing in the sky that night.

Lying on her back in the bathroom on the cool of the white marble tiles, she heard the summons again. Her husband tapped the horn of the car: one long, noisy beep followed by two shorter taps, as if in apology. She strained to close the zipper on a pair of jeans without pinching the soft flesh of her midsection. It was a task she found both onerous and humiliating, primarily since she had purchased the pair less than a month ago, having gone through the same depressing experience with every other pair that lay folded in her dresser. Another short beep to remind her (in case she had forgotten) that her husband and daughter were waiting in the idling car, but this really had been sprung on her, and there might be photos. She wanted to at least make an attempt at presentability. There weren't many photos of the two of them anymore, not like the early days, before Charlotte was born. Now any photo seemed to be taken from their six-year-old daughter's height—hardly a flattering angle: the upward tilt of Greta's crooked smile, and the heavy lower lids of Phillip's distracted and vaguely startled eyes, as though he didn't quite expect to find himself there.

Finally she managed to maneuver the zipper most of the way but left the top button unbuttoned. She pulled her oversized T-shirt over it and grabbed a sweater on her way out the door, stuffed it into her bag, and ran to the car. Phillip had backed it out of the driveway and waited at the curb.

"Sorry," she said through the open window.

"We're going to miss it, Mama!" Charlotte pouted.

Greta glanced at her daughter strapped into the backseat, still dressed in her pink gymnastic unitard and flip-flops. The air had begun to cool and Greta could see the gooseflesh on Charlotte's skinny arms.

"Did you pack her a sweater?" Greta asked Phillip.

"I thought you did. Isn't that what was taking so long?"

Greta didn't answer, ashamed that she had packed a sweater for herself but not for Charlotte.

"I can go back," she said, but Phillip was already driving down the street, away from children's sweaters and dinner half-prepared. She tried to remember if she had locked the door behind her but figured that they would be gone for such a short amount of time, the chances of a break-in were unlikely.

"I'm not cold," Charlotte insisted. She had her legs stretched out onto Phillip's seat in front of her.

"I know, honey, but we aren't outside. Put your feet down."

Charlotte dropped her legs in a dramatic fashion. "*Daddy* lets me."

Greta studied the side of her husband's face. Squinting into the sun, he almost looked as though he were smiling. But his jaw was rigid. Greta could tell that he was grinding his teeth and thought about reminding him of the warning their dentist had given Phillip at his annual checkup but decided against it. He careened down the hill, running through yellow lights on their way to the ocean. Charlotte made excited noises that increased in volume with each turn.

"Whoaaaaa . . . whoaaaa!" She exaggerated with the movement of her body as though they were thundering along a roller-coaster track.

"What do you think, the ocean or the mountains?" Phillip asked.

"Well, I hope the ocean because that's where we're headed," Greta said.

Phillip glanced over at her, did a quick inventory of her face, and then looked back at the road.

"I mean, this is your thing," she said. "I didn't even know anything about it."

"They only happen every twenty years," he said quietly. "It seems like a shame not to at least make the effort."

"That means that the next time there's a harvest moon, I'll be a grown-up!" Charlotte told her mother. "Right, Daddy?"

"That's right, sweetheart." Phillip smiled at her in the rear-view mirror. Greta watched the lines appear around his eyes and along the sides of his mouth as he smiled. It made his face look like it was melting, softening, but then just as quickly his jaw set and the determination reappeared.

"What makes this one so special is the fact that it's so close to the equinox," Phillip explained in a louder voice so that his daughter could hear him from the backseat. "Usually it's days, or maybe even weeks apart, but this time it's only six hours!"

"'Equinox,'" Charlotte repeated gravely.

Greta was sure her daughter didn't know the word. She turned around and said, "Equinox means when day and night are about the same length."

"I KNOW!" her daughter screamed. Phillip startled and the car swerved slightly into the other lane and then back again.

Greta grabbed onto the dashboard, hitting an imaginary brake with her foot. "Jesus Christ!" She ran her hands through her hair, grabbing little fistfuls of it.

"Charlotte!" Phillip said, raising his voice.

"You *told* me already, Daddy! She's always telling me things I already know." Charlotte pointed at her mother accusingly, and when both parents were silent, at a loss for words, she started to whimper for effect.

"It's true, I did tell her," Phillip said to Greta in a low voice intended only for her. "While we were in the driveway."

Greta waited for Phillip to discipline Charlotte. Paternal authority always carried more weight—though perhaps it only seemed this way to Greta, since it had been the case in her own childhood home—but when Phillip failed to say anything, Greta turned around to lecture her daughter herself.

Charlotte was no longer trying to cry, her tiny shoulders folded inward with an approximation of sadness, but staring at a bug scuttling across the windowpane beside her. She watched it in silence, patiently and oddly still. Just as the bug reached the edge of the glass, Charlotte reached out her little hand and squashed it with her thumb. Greta half expected her to lick it off like their big overweight tabby would have done. Bile rose up from her stomach to the top of her throat, shocking her. She clamped her hand over her mouth.

"Stop the car!" she tried to yell, but with the bile flooding into her mouth and her hand pressed tight to her lips, the words were indecipherable.

Phillip pulled over to the side of the road, and Greta lurched out of the car before he came to a complete stop. She took her hand away from her mouth and spit onto the ground. The ocean air slapped her skin and whipped her hair around her face. Hunched over, she waited to see if there was anything more to come, but all she had was the sour taste in her mouth.

She could hear Charlotte's muffled voice coming from the backseat, asking Phillip if Mama was okay. The blood rushed to Greta's head and she straightened up slowly, feeling dizzy. When she looked across the beach parking lot and up at the darkening sky, she couldn't see the moon. If it was there, it was covered in the heavy low-slung ocean mist.

Phillip got out of the car and told Charlotte to stay where she was. Greta watched the overgrown palm trees swaying in the breeze. She had always felt a sort of kinship with the palm trees, transported here from somewhere else. Having grown up outside of Seattle, Greta was accustomed to her oceans surrounded by the great majestic cedar trees of the Pacific Northwest.

"What happened?" Phillip said, skirting along the gravel. He reached Greta and placed his hand on her shoulder.

She shrugged. "Could be the hormone shots. It's a possible side effect," she said.

He took his hand off of her shoulder and brushed the hair away from her face. It nearly made her cry from the tenderness. A tenderness long absent, but somehow unnoticeable until it's back—even the smallest taste of it.

"I hate to break it to you," she said, trying to smile. "But I don't think there's any moon tonight. Harvest or otherwise."

He scanned the sky, searching for a sign of the moon. The setting sun cast a reddish glow over everything, briefly turning his blond hair rosy-colored, like the frosted pink mane of one of their daughter's stuffed ponies. Greta giggled at the image. Phillip glanced at her with annoyance. "We're missing it," he said.

"I'm sorry," she said. She tried to assume the right expression, the patient, wifely expression that would say, even though this isn't my fault, I'll accept the blame.

"I guess we should have gone to the mountains." He sighed.

Greta took his hand and laced her fingers through his. "We still can. It's not all the way dark yet. Why don't we do that?"

Opening the door for Greta, he kissed her quickly on the forehead and headed around to the driver's side.

"Charlotte has her violin lesson," he said. "Theresa's probably already at the house waiting."

"Theresa!" Charlotte shrieked with excitement.

"I didn't even know that you scheduled a violin lesson. Didn't she already have one this week?"

"It's on the calendar," Phillip said. "All you have to do is check it."

He shifted the car into drive and signaled to the oncoming cars that he wanted in. Greta craned her head to help him look. It was a habit that Phillip had first teased her about, citing it as a lack of confidence in his driving. Then he had cajoled, criticized, and finally flat-out asked her not to do it. Despite his insistence, even now she could not stop herself. Though why she thought she was any more capable than her husband at spotting danger, or opportunity, Greta couldn't say.

Greta had found Theresa on Craigslist two years earlier. A student from the Berklee College of Music, Theresa had originally intended to take a semester off, but that had stretched into a year, and now almost two. Greta had always assumed it was because of a boy, but Theresa had never mentioned anyone. Then again, Theresa had barely spoken to Greta since that first lesson when Greta had asked if a check was okay or if she preferred cash. Not that Theresa seemed even remotely concerned about money. She took the thirty-five dollars from Greta with barely a nod and stuffed it into her back pocket. Greta wondered how often she forgot the money there—how many times she found the bills and peeled them dark and wet out of her jeans before they went through the dryer.

All that Greta knew about Theresa was that she lived with an older sister and her older sister's boyfriend, Grady Rizcoff, in Venice. Grady Rizcoff was a musician who'd had marginal success as a drummer in an early '90s grunge band. The band's success stalled after the lead singer overdosed, found Jesus, and subsequently refused to write the kind of music that had put them on the charts. Greta wasn't sure what Theresa's sister did. She was either a waitress or the manager of her boyfriend's career, possibly both.

Theresa taught violin to a handful of children, including Charlotte. According to her résumé, she was one of the youngest people to have attended Berklee, matriculating at age seventeen, but now she didn't seem to have much motivation to return.

She was standing on the front step with her violin case in hand and a single iPod headphone in her ear when Phillip pulled the car into the driveway. Charlotte burst out of the car and threw her arms around Theresa's slender frame.

"Sorry we're late," Phillip called out of the window as he switched off the ignition. "We got stuck on an errand."

"We were looking for the harvest moon!" Charlotte told her. "There's one every twenty years!" Theresa took off her purple Wayfarers and propped them up on top of her head. She knelt down and ruffled Charlotte's hair.

"How's my girl?" she murmured. Everything Theresa said sounded like a murmur to Greta.

Charlotte lunged for Theresa, clamping her body around her like a marsupial and knocking her off balance.

"Charlotte!" Greta said.

Charlotte released Theresa and sprinted up the steps to the house.

"Come on, Theresa!" she yelled over her shoulder.

Theresa stood up and smoothed out the back of her jeans.

"You could have just gone right in," Greta said. "I don't think we even locked it." She didn't know why she said this. The thought of having anyone in her house while she wasn't there wasn't especially desirable. "We were on one of Phillip's 'commando missions,'" she added, smiling.

Theresa smiled back at her. It always took Greta by surprise how this timid and mild and slightly uncomfortable-looking girl would suddenly come alive with that smile. It illuminated her face, lifting it out of the mundane and into something radiant.

"It's really okay, really," Theresa said. "I was enjoying the sunset."

Greta nodded and then absently looked at her watch. They weren't late at all, she noticed. They were early.

Charlotte practiced chromatic scales and arpeggios with clear and confident agility. Occasionally, Theresa's bowing could be heard instructing and harmonizing and the sound of the two playing together echoed throughout the lofty house, bouncing off the tall walls and into the kitchen where Greta was preparing dinner. Once it was in the oven and two places had been set, Greta laid out the myriad hormone drugs on the kitchen table, the Follistim, Lupron, and Clomid, the two different syringes, and the red plastic container with the alarming illustration of a skull and crossbones and black lettering on the side, warning, HAZARDOUS WASTE. HANDLE WITH CARE.

She took out the black-and-white composition book where she had scribbled extensive notes while the nurse at her fertility specialist's practice had told her which shot to administer, when, and in which order. Considering that this was to be their third and—after a lengthy and alternately logical and emotional debate—the mutually agreed-upon *last* try, it was frustrating that the drugs were as bewildering and the self-administered shots as harrowing as the first time. At least once a week she relied on a homemade YouTube video of a woman with rosacea-flushed skin expertly mixing the drugs and giving them to herself with the exhibitionist zeal commonly found in IVF veterans. Phillip walked into the kitchen just as Greta gave herself the last shot in her thigh.

"Ow," he said. He shielded the side of his face with his hand. From the beginning, Phillip had been explicit in his refusal to have anything to do with the shots.

"I'll masturbate in the plastic cups, I'll let them count my sperm as many times as they want, but no needles," he had announced.

Greta had laughed. "Such a sacrifice. Really? You'll masturbate in a plastic cup for me?"

"For her," he had said, drawing a ring around her belly with his index finger.

"Another girl?" she had teased. "What's wrong with a boy? Haven't you had enough estrogen for one lifetime?"

"You would think, wouldn't you," he had said, stretching himself across her while they breathed each other in.

———————

Twenty-two months and three tries later, they didn't talk about the possible genders anymore. Nor did they discuss VBACS, epidurals, hospital versus birthing centers, or whether doulas really were worth the cost or not. Now Greta tried to shield him from everything about the process in an attempt to make it all appear as effortless as possible.

He walked over to the oven and peered inside. "Hello, lasagna," he said. "Aren't you cute."

Greta recorded the amount of hormones she had injected, broke off the tips of the syringes, and stuffed them into the red disposal box. Then she put everything in the wicker pie basket her mother gave her years ago, still unused for its intended purpose but surprisingly handy for this one.

"Did you finish packing?" she asked. "I laid the shirts I picked up at the cleaners on your dresser."

"I packed them, thanks."

Charlotte's scales increased in speed. Phillip walked to the doorway and cocked his head, listening.

"She's getting pretty good, isn't she?" he said.

Greta walked to the cupboard and replaced the basket. "I don't know. I can't tell. They're just scales."

"I mean, I think there's been some noticeable improvement since we've added the extra lessons," Phillip said. He listened for another moment with his eyes closed until the scales stopped and there was quiet. "Theresa said Charlie's one of the most naturally gifted students she's had," he added.

"Coming from a nineteen-year-old music-school dropout, that's high praise."

It came out before the thought had fully formed in her mind. But it was out, and Greta scrambled to come up with something that would soften the edges.

"It's nice that she likes it so much," Greta said finally. She sat back at the table and looked at her husband.

Phillip leaned against the kitchen counter and idly began to organize the various objects—prized flea-market finds, old medicine bottles, ashtrays from long-shuttered hotels—in horizontal lines. He nodded steadily as though listening to a song in his head. She watched him go far, far away from her, and then snap back.

"Hey, I wanted to let you know that I'll do the long-term parking. I don't want you driving me to the airport so early."

"I don't mind. If we put her in the back, she'll fall right back asleep."

"No, you can use the sleep. And the company will cover it." He walked over to where Greta was sitting and kissed the top of her head.

"Christ, your hair smells good," he said.

"What does it smell like?" she asked, eager for the compliment.

"Apples," he said after taking another long inhalation. "Green apples." He turned to go, but she grabbed his hand.

"Don't leave," she said.

"It's just for three days."

She pulled him close, wrapping her arms around his waist and pressing her cheek to his stomach. It didn't seem fair that his stomach remained firm and hard while hers softened as the hormones accelerated her body into thinking it had to conceive.

"No, I mean don't leave *right now*. This second. We never have any time without Charlotte . . ."

"And yet, you want to do it all again."

She drew back from him and looked up at his face.

"'You'? Don't you mean *us*? Or is this divine conception we're talking about?"

"Us," he corrected.

Charlotte's hasty steps ricocheted down the hallway and into the kitchen as she bounded into the room, stopping at the sight of her parents embracing.

"I saw that," she said, with a knowing look. It was a habit she had picked up the same month she had turned five. Greta wondered where. At a playdate? Did she hear someone else say it? What did the kids talk about all day at that strange neighborhood Montessori school?

Following at a short distance behind, Theresa approached the kitchen. She paused at the doorway, shifting her weight from foot to foot as if awaiting permission to enter. It was exasperating to Greta, and straining to hide her annoyance, she motioned for Theresa to come in. It seemed to Greta that Theresa was one of those girls who spent all of her time being an imposition while obviously trying *not* to be an imposition. Almost everything Theresa said or did broadcast the message "I won't take it for myself. You'll have to give it to me." So Greta felt perpetually obliged to invite her to sit down, offer her food, and question her about her life, only to receive the same elusive and monosyllabic answers. Their conversations inevitably dwindled into silence within minutes.

"Those scales sounded great!" Greta said.

"Her fingering is getting much more confident—can you hear it?" Theresa murmured.

"I can *definitely* hear it," Phillip said. He grabbed Charlotte and hugged her close as she flailed for show. "You are my brilliant girl." He extravagantly kissed the top of her head and then opened his arms to let her free. She lurched forward and then flung herself back into his embrace as he closed his arms around her in a familiar display of their father-daughter choreography.

Greta was anxious to finish their dinner. She had deliberately fed Charlotte early to give her and Phillip the chance to have dinner by themselves. Their daughter's long and arduous march to bedtime was looming ahead and with Phillip leaving in the morning, she desperately wanted at least fifteen minutes alone with him before the hormone drugs put her to sleep. These days, the mere touch of her cheek on the cotton pillowcase made her eyes heavy. She knew that she should invite Theresa to dinner—it's what she had learned in the house she grew up in, where anyone who dropped by unexpectedly was given their own place at the table before they were even asked. And knowing that Theresa would decline, there was even more reason to offer. But she *might* say yes. There was a chance, however minuscule, and Greta didn't want to take it.

"I'll walk you out to your car," Phillip said to Theresa.

As Theresa quietly followed Phillip down the hall to the front door, Charlotte scrambled to her feet and ran after them. It was at this late hour, when she was punchy and tired, that Charlotte became wildly unaware of where her personal space ended. Her arms became elastic and floundering, and she ran too fast, inevitably failing to see the edge of the table, the corner angle of the hallway, or the slick bathroom tiles. Recently Greta had rifled through Charlotte's bedroom to find her sticker collection so she could apply them to all of the plate glass windows, out of fear that, if they were left unmarked, her daughter would fly right through them one night.

"Theresa," Charlotte called out as she ran, "I want to hug you good-bye!"

Greta got up and followed them, arriving at the front door just as Charlotte threw herself at Theresa. She collided against her with so much force that Greta heard Theresa take a little involuntary breath. She staggered back a step, accidentally dropping her violin. Somehow Phillip caught it before it hit the floor.

"Easy, Charlotte, easy now," he said, holding the violin and motioning for his daughter to disengage herself.

"See you next week, Lottie," Theresa murmured. It was a nickname that Greta had never used, but what surprised her the most was the lack of reaction from Charlotte. It must not have been the first time her daughter had heard it.

"Okay, that's enough," Phillip said, touching Charlotte on the shoulder. "You'll see her very soon. Say good-bye now."

But Charlotte only grabbed on tighter. Theresa laughed nervously. She looked to Phillip with a helpless widening of the eyes.

Greta noticed Phillip's expression hardening, Greta's signal to intervene.

"Charlotte," Greta said, her voice raised. "I'm going to count to three, and then there will be a consequence. One . . . two . . ."

Just before Greta reached three, Charlotte released Theresa. Then she tipped forward on her toes and very quickly and deliberately kissed Theresa's breasts—first the left, then the right. Theresa gasped and instinctively crossed her arms to cover her chest. Her face flushed as she looked apologetically at Greta and Phillip and then down, clearly disoriented by their daughter.

Both parents were stunned. Charlotte looked at them, challenging with a smile.

"*Charlotte!*" Phillip yelled. But before he could say anything else, she had raced off to her room. They heard the door slam behind her. "What the fuck?" he said to Greta.

"I'll deal with it," she told Phillip. "Sorry, Theresa. I don't know what is going on with her."

Theresa smiled and waved her hand dismissively "Kids love me," she said.

"Come on, I'll walk you out," Phillip said as he glanced back at Greta. "I'll be just a minute."

Greta set off down the hallway, preparing to initiate the long slumbering process, calculating in her mind just how many books she was required to read before she could turn off the light and lie with her husband in their own bed.

Phillip returned minutes later and interrupted Charlotte's supervised teeth brushing with the news that Theresa had accidentally locked her keys in her car.

"I don't understand. How did she—"

"They were in her purse," he said. "She forgot."

"Does she have Triple-A or . . ." Greta trailed off, noticing that Phillip already had the keys to the Volvo in his hand. "You aren't driving her home, are you?"

Charlotte jumped up and down with her mouth full of toothpaste. "Can I come? Can I come?"

Greta put her hand on her daughter's shoulder and directed her back to the bathroom sink. Charlotte cupped her little hands together, rinsed her mouth, and spat.

"Her sister has a spare key, but she's stuck at the house and can't come over."

"I wanna come!" Charlotte pleaded. She ran over to her father and stood on his feet with her own.

"Sorry, sweetheart. It's past your bedtime. Next time, I promise."

"Mean Daddy!" Charlotte shrieked. She ran out of the bedroom and down the hall to her own room, slamming the door once again.

He sighed and turned off the faucet that Charlotte had left running.

"Phillip! You're leaving in the morning! Couldn't she take a cab?" Greta tried to sound reasonable but failed to disguise the neediness in her own voice.

"It's not far. I'll be back before you even have a chance to wash your face," he said, and quickly kissed her. "Don't you dare fall asleep without me!"

Mother and daughter curled up limb over limb next to each other in the narrow twin bed. Hair had been brushed, books read, closets checked for monsters, and nightlights strategically placed around the room. Greta ran her fingers through Charlotte's hair and tried to keep up her end of the conversation while her eyes ached with fatigue. She wondered if Phillip had left Theresa's sister's house yet and if he would try to multitask on the way home—use every moment wisely, as his consultant brain told him (and often told her). Pick up bread, Saran Wrap, and two-percent milk from the local twenty-four-hour supermarket. He might try to buy an early edition of the *Wall Street Journal* or the *Times*, even though he could get either of these online; for years now he still insisted on buying the print edition. "I like the dirtiness of the ink on my fingers." She remembered him saying this to her in grad school, when he was getting his MBA, and how it would never fail to make her hot and embarrassed.

Charlotte reached up under Greta's arm and scratched the back of her neck.

"And what if I grew extra arms and legs, and they were furry like a spider, would you still love me then?" Charlotte asked.

"Yes, I would," Greta answered, though there was really no need to. This wasn't a game about answers but about questions. How outrageous, unpleasant, and fearsome could we become and still be loved?

Charlotte snuggled into Greta deeper. "Okay," Greta said, "Two more, then I'm going to my bed."

"Where's Daddy? I want a Daddy snuggle, too."

"Not tonight, honey. He'll come give you a kiss when he gets home."

Charlotte's body went rigid for a moment, preparing for a fight, but then she yawned as exhaustion overpowered the desire to protest.

"And what if . . . I had a nose like this?" Charlotte took her little finger and smushed her nose down and a bit to the side. "Like this *all* the time . . . or, no. Just on Tuesdays." She lifted her head up for Greta's inspection and frowned when she saw that her eyes were closed. "Mama, you have to look!" Greta opened her eyes halfway and glanced at her daughter.

"Well, since it's only on Tuesdays . . ."

"No, *all* the time," Charlotte emended the question.

"Yes, I would still love you." Greta sighed and closed her eyes again. "One more, honey, so make it a good one."

Charlotte was silent for a moment. Greta could feel the sleep beginning to overtake her. She tried to breathe in the same rhythm as her daughter, to make as little noise as possible so as to gently lull her to sleep. The trick was to get her to sleep without falling asleep herself. She hoped to be able to take a bath and change into something pretty. Maybe the sheer cotton lace nightgown that Phillip bought her in Spain during that long-ago year they took off from school together. He had seen her fingering the lace trim and asking the old woman the cost in her halting Spanish before putting it back on the rack. It was more money than she allowed herself to spend on clothes in those days. Not with more than a hundred grand in student loans and the cost of the wedding they were hoping to save up for. While she was at the *pensione* taking a nap, Phillip had found his way back through the maze of the Andalusian streets to the tiny store and bought the nightgown. He presented it to her with such boyish pride when she woke up that her heart swelled with her love of him. She put the garment on just for him to take off.

Oh God, how she missed him. How she missed the closeness in the years before Charlotte, when they would excite each other with only a look, a word, or a promise of what they would do to each other later—after class or after a party. Those days when they would come at each other breathless from the sheer force of their desire and make love until their bodies rebelled against them, leaving the two trembling and happy and raw.

Charlotte's sleepy voice jarred her back to the present.

"And what if . . . I didn't love you? Would you still love me?"

The question puzzled Greta. She looked at her daughter in profile. How much she looked like him! The fair skin and the freckles and even the exact same blue vein across her forehead.

The slender nose and the green-and-blue sea-glass eyes and the eyelashes curled to blond tips. There seemed to be virtually nothing of her in her daughter's face that she recognized as her own. Not that it should matter, of course. She had read somewhere that offspring resemble the father at birth so that he has visible proof of paternity and won't abandon the child or, worse, attack it. Charlotte was living proof of Phillip's virility. She was a carbon copy of him. Could this be an obscure motivation for wanting to do it again, to create a child that looked like her instead of her husband? Could she possibly be that narcissistic?

Greta and Phillip had tried unsuccessfully to have a second child since Charlotte was two. Their failure was surprising to both of them since they had conceived their daughter within weeks of Greta's stopping birth-control pills. It didn't seem possible after all that time trying *not* to get pregnant to suddenly try and then fail. But as months and then years passed, they finally had to accept that they were going to be one of those statistics. They briefly considered adoption, but Greta worried about the possibility of favoring their biological child. Greta's mother had been raised by a stepfather who treated her half siblings with far more indulgence and care, and Greta could never quite silence her mother's voice intoning, "Better to have *all* adopted children—don't mix the two."

The transition to assisted conception was gradual. They bought books that Phillip diligently highlighted with questions for the doctors. Greta learned about checking her cervical fluid and making fertility charts. They took her basal body temperature and made love according to its fluctuations. The

doctors started Greta on low doses of Clomid, and several at-
tempts of the "turkey baster" were all met with no success. By
the time they prepared to try in-vitro fertilization, they were
already so stressed-out and exhausted that they silently dreaded
it. They would wait in the doctor's waiting room like weary
warriors on the sidelines of a battle that already seemed to be
lost.

"Important to keep positive outlook!" their first doctor's
Chinese nurse practitioner would tell Greta while she searched
for a vein to take blood. Chin Lau Wong was fond of quoting
inspirational aphorisms to keep her patients' spirits up. "If you
are in hurry, you never get there," or "A journey of a thousand
miles begin with single step." When Greta repeated one of
these platitudes to Phillip, flawlessly imitating the accent for
laughs, Phillip told her that Chin Lau Wong should shut the
fuck up and write for a greeting-card company. The rancor and
dismissal of her husband's reply stunned her. They had always
made each other laugh in the worst of times. It was one of the
things that she felt they relied upon when everything else
faltered—when his parents died or when her nephew went
missing and they found out he had been doing heroin since
dropping out of school at fifteen. The only thing dependable in
times such as these was the comfort of their love, the thing that
she believed in above all else.

She realized at that moment that she had never answered
Charlotte's question.

"Yes. I would love you," she whispered into her daughter's
hair. "Even if you didn't love me. I would always love you."

What is it that keeps us in fear of revelation? By whose design it is that we are held, suspended, hovering over our own lives? Bearing witness to it, yes, but not remembering. Choosing *not* to remember. The shy glances, the nervous tenor, the new gym membership, the unnecessary errands. What keeps us from noticing? Or if noticing, then not telling ourselves that these details matter. We need to pay attention. Because if we don't . . . then what?

What is it that keeps us safe from what we know, *should* know to be true? Is it really ignorance, or is it a sort of kindness that we give to ourselves? A part of us takes over. *Just put it off until we're stronger*, it would say if it had a voice that we could hear. *You're not ready yet. You're not ready. Let everyone else see it but not me. Spare me this. Please, not this.*

It was past three in the morning when Greta awoke to the sound of the shower running. She was alone in bed. Twice already during the night, she had reached her arm across to Phillip's side and found it empty. She had thought about getting up and going into his office, where he was probably working on the case as he often did before he left on business, but the bed was so warm and Charlotte would certainly be up at six and demanding her attention. At least, that's what she had told herself.

She got out of bed and walked to the bathroom. Phillip was standing in the shower with his eyes closed, hot water streaming over his head. The moon shone down on him directly from the skylight above, and his pale skin looked even paler in the light. She stared at him, thinking that he looked like something holy.

He opened his eyes and gasped at the sight of her.

"Jesus!" he said, and put his palm over the left side of his chest, over his heart. "You're awake."

"So are you." Greta stood just outside the open tiled shower in her cotton nightgown. If he noticed that it was *the* nightgown, he gave no indication. He took the bar of soap, lathered it up between his hands, and then ran it over his body, turning away from her as he washed between his legs.

"You were sound asleep when I got home," he said to her over his shoulder. "I hope I didn't wake you up."

He put the soap back, but it slid out of the holder and hit the floor and found its place on the drain. He left it there.

"What time did you get home?" she said. "I tried to stay up reading for a while after I put Charlotte to bed, but—"

"How is she?"

"She's fine."

"Good, good," he said.

Greta pulled the nightgown up over her head and let it fall to the floor. She stood for a moment and waited for him to take in the sight of her naked body. He looked at her, smiled dimly, then looked away.

"Can I join you?" she asked as she entered the shower without invitation.

"I'm almost done," he said, stepping aside.

She bent down and picked up the bar of soap.

"Let me do your back," she said. She rubbed the soap over his broad shoulders and along his back, then put the soap aside and ran her bare hands over his warm, slick skin. Her hands traveled around his sides and down his stomach and found his penis. It was soft and wet. She cupped it in her hands as she would a small and delicate animal.

"I'm really tired," he said by way of apology.

She took her hands away and turned him around to face her.

"It's okay, honey. We're not supposed to anyway."

"Right."

"And remember while you're away, no—"

"I know," he said. She noticed the edge in his voice.

"Hey." She put her hands up to his face. "Don't do that," she said.

"I'm sorry." He took a deep breath. "I'm just really, really tired."

"I know," she said. "Did you prepare the presentation?"

"Mostly," he said.

"Mostly?" She stepped back and looked at him. "It's after three in the—"

"I mean *yes*," he said. "It's a hard one, and some of the data is just . . . The details are unclear and . . ."

He trailed off, shaking his head. Suddenly, he pulled her to him and embraced her.

"It's okay," she said. "I'm sure that once you get in there and sit down with them, all of the—"

It was then that she noticed that his body was shaking.

"Phillip?" she said, but he only held her tighter. She saw the tears now, and it scared her. It was such a rare occurrence for Phillip to cry; the last time was when Charlotte fell off the monkey bars at school and briefly lost consciousness. When Greta had finally managed to get through to Phillip's international cell phone and tell him that the tests had come back as only a "slight concussion" and that he didn't need to fly home, he started crying so violently that he had to pull to the side of the road.

"I'm sorry," he said. "I'm so sorry."

"For what?" Greta asked.

He didn't answer.

"For what?" she repeated.

The water started to run cold. She reached her arm out from under his and turned the handle to the left. Phillip's eyes were bloodshot, the sea-glass irises sharp and bright in contrast to the red.

"Everything is going to be okay," she told him.

He grasped on to her tighter.

"Do you hear me?" she said.

"Yes." His voice sounded very small. "Oh God," he said, and started to speak, but the words caught in his throat. "I'm sorry, I don't know what's wrong with me, I . . ."

"It doesn't matter," she said. "It's all going to be all right. Do you understand?" Greta was surprised by the authority she heard in her own voice. "It's all going to be all right."

She repeated it again.

And again and again and again.

REDBUD

ILSE O'HARA CLOSED HER EYES when her daughter Greta cut across two lanes of traffic and swung a U-turn to secure the parking place in front of the nursery. For years, Ilse had refused to let any of her children drive her, but now as she found herself fading into that increasing invisibility of the elderly, she no longer bothered protesting being relegated to the passenger seat.

"You know that's illegal," she said. She would sit it the passenger seat, but that didn't mean that she would keep quiet.

"Yeah," Greta said. "But if I didn't do it, we'd get stuck. They won't let you do a U-turn for miles." Greta turned down the radio to concentrate and expertly backed into the spot. "And look at this. It's the Ko!"

"The what?" Ilse peered out the window at the espaliered apple trees trained beside the entrance. Although she had always admired the art, along with bonsai, she couldn't help but feel that there was something cruelly manipulative about it. She

supposed that you could argue that all landscaping was ma-
nipulation of a kind, but these trees looked crippled, like the
victims of Chinese foot binding.

"The Ko," Greta said. "You know, as in the Kojak?"

"You mean the bald man?" Ilse narrowed her eyes and
frowned at having lost the thread of conversation. "I don't understand."

Greta attempted to explain the concept: in college, her
friends used to refer to ideal parking spaces as the "the Kojak"
because in the 1970s television series, the main character would
inevitably pull into an empty parking spot just in front of the
location where he was about to bust the bad guy. "Get it? The
Kojak. Or, for short, the Ko."

"Kojak was Greek," Ilse said as she carefully climbed down
out of the SUV. Why everyone felt the need to drive these
enormous gas–guzzling monstrosities was beyond her. She drove
all three of her children in a powder-blue 1966 Chevrolet just
fine, but now everyone's car was bigger, fatter, and taller,
blocking your view of the road and forcing you to succumb
and purchase a big ridiculous car yourself. It was like being in
a restaurant where some loudmouth decides to raise his voice,
and everyone else raises theirs in turn in order to be heard.
After a while, it becomes a cacophony of dinner conversations
that no one wants to hear.

While Greta rifled through her purse for change for the
parking meter, Ilse walked to the back of the car and examined
the dents on the bumper. All of her children were terrible drivers. Well, her daughters. It was ironic that her son, the only

good driver, had died behind the wheel. He had been just shy of his twenty-second birthday at the time of the accident, and though ultimately it was deemed a suicide, Ilse still believed that Rory didn't really want to die. He wanted to live; only, he could never truly figure out how.

"They weren't me," Greta said, gesturing to the dents.

"It's not going to help the resale any," Ilse said.

"Well, then I guess it's a good thing I'm not selling it," Greta said. It was impossible to be with her mother for any length of time without reverting to their old mother-daughter animosity—something that began in Greta's teen years. At age thirty-nine, however, Greta understood that this antagonism was no longer just a phase, as she had once hoped it would be, but something that would remain throughout her life, like a chronic stiffening of the bones. As much as Greta would have liked it, they would never revert back to the easy comfort she had once felt as her mother's last child, her "change of life" baby. Greta grew up far too early, and for this she felt she was never entirely forgiven.

Ilse sighed, giving Greta the eerie impression, as she often did, of her mother listening to her thoughts.

"Is this place even open?" Ilse said. "It doesn't look open to me."

As she shuffled across the gravel, Ilse took off her prescription sunglasses and replaced them with her trifocals. She stood at the entrance of the nursery and examined a row of succulents. Greta strode past her into the entrance.

"It's open," she said, waiting for Ilse to join her.

"I never much cared for cactuses," Ilse said.

"Cacti," Greta corrected.

"Cacti," Ilse repeated. It was one of her daughter's most maddening traits, her quickness to point out when Ilse was wrong. She knew it was "cacti" the moment she said "cactuses"—of course it was "cacti"—but Greta was so fast in correcting her that Ilse hadn't had the chance to do it herself. She thought of all of the times her own mother made a mess of her English grammar, yet Ilse had never dared to correct her. Her mother was already in her early twenties when, with only the barest knowledge of English, she had emigrated from Germany. Her first husband and Ilse's birth father, Gunther, had died early in the war, and by the time the kind, curly-haired Irish-American soldier showed up in their village just south of Düsseldorf and fell for Ilse's mother, she was all too happy to be claimed. The fact that she had a three-year-old daughter didn't seem to diminish the soldier's ardor at all—at least, not yet. It didn't hurt that Ilse was an exceptionally beautiful child. She had inherited her father's rosy-cheeked complexion, and her hair, as pale as the wheat fields surrounding their village, hung in elegant natural curls around her fine-boned face. It took less than a year, after the hastily formed family arrived in the Pacific Northwest, for Ilse's mother to learn rudimentary English. Determined to allay the obvious discomfort of her new husband's family, she spoke only English from the moment she moved into the forbidding, drafty Victorian home; whenever Ilse tried to speak German with her mother, she was either hushed or ignored. As a consequence, before she had even turned six, Ilse

had surpassed her mother in English, and despite her early ef-
forts, Ilse's mother would speak a heavily accented broken
English for the rest of her life. Yet she lived without fear of
challenge, whereas Ilse's own daughter never failed to correct
Ilse's grammar or pronunciation.

Greta waited for her mother at the entrance with a spiral notebook in hand. She had asked her mother to come and help with
a new landscaping project, and now she was trying hard not to
regret it. Ilse was an expert amateur botanist; any house that
she had lived in had possessed a lush and wild garden. Bursting
forth in all directions, her gardens were so remarkable in their
untamed beauty that strangers often stopped by the house to
admire them. A local Oregon paper once even sent a reporter
to interview her mother, photographing her posing awkwardly
next to a row of heirloom tomatoes—this well before the proliferation of everything heirloom at the local farmers' markets.
Much of the charm of these gardens arose from such pockets of
exoticism. Throughout Greta's childhood, her mother had
steadfastly refused to grow anything standard. How Greta had
longed for a classic Red Delicious apple or a perfectly round
beefsteak tomato as a child, but Ilse had insisted that these were
for the ordinary. It seemed to Greta that Ilse was a perfectionist
who coveted the imperfect. The quote the paper ran to accom-
pany the photo was "There is no such thing as a green thumb.
Only people willing to get brown knees." Greta remembered
how proud she had been of her mother's aphorism, assuming
that she had coined the phrase, only to see it years later embroidered on a pillow in a mail-order catalog.

Although it was true that Greta had taken on the new terrace garden project, calling on her mother's aid was mostly a pretext, what her husband had always referred to as her tendency to "bait and switch." A few days earlier, her mother had casually mentioned over the phone that she and Greta's father had agreed to take in Greta's sister's son Milo who, at twenty-two, had announced that he was serious about getting off drugs. It had taken considerable effort on Ilse's part to get Milo to even consider coming to live with his grandparents on the tiny Pacific Northwest island where they had more or less retired, but it seemed that life in the Los Angeles suburb where Milo had been raised by Greta's older sister, Laurel, and her string of unsuitable men, had become untenable. He ran away from home for the first time when he was fourteen years old, choosing to live with the mild if vacuous cannabis-dealing parents of his girlfriend, Summer. By the time he was fifteen, the girlfriend had moved on to an older man she met at a local minimall coffee bar, and the pseudofamily, no longer interested in sympathizing with Milo or discrediting his mother, from whom he had been growing impossibly estranged, kicked him out of their house. The last thing Summer's mother had said to him after he had waited on the front porch for hours for her to return was, "Milo, you will never be able to take care of Summer, and she will never be able to take care of herself. You must let her go." That night, he tried heroin for the first time in a stranger's garage and imagined that he was a baby again in Laurel's arms before everything went bad.

Greta couldn't help but judge her sister harshly as a parent. Laurel had Milo when she was in her early twenties, and it seemed to Greta that she spent Milo's childhood distractedly pursuing a replacement father for the one that Milo—and Laurel—never really knew. By the time he was nine years old, Milo was so angry at Laurel for not being there, for choosing other men over him, that he became a master of the insult. He disparaged Laurel for everything. She couldn't cook or clean; she was forgetful, clumsy, careless; and she had no money. She didn't even have a college education, as he was quick to remind her, especially in front of a suitor. Why would you want to be with her, he asked, if you didn't have to? He wore her down with his relentless reproaches and punishing judgments until she found herself actually hoping, when he walked out of their apartment at the age of fourteen, that he wouldn't come back. This was confessed to Greta one night after too much wine, hastily retracted, and never spoken of again.

And now it had been over a year since Laurel had become entrenched in a New Age yoga practice—"a cult," their father insisted, despite other higher courts deeming it a "new religion." Whatever it was, it was clear to Greta that it took Laurel away from her sorrow, from her son, and most of all from the question of what she would do with her life which, at age forty-four, had transformed into the question of what she *hadn't* done with her life. The "self-realization" she had recently experienced was a balm for all of the feelings of failure, imbuing her with a sense of direction and purpose that she claimed not to have felt since she was pregnant with Milo. All of the meddling and overbearing instruction that she had steadfastly rejected from their parents Laurel welcomed from the religion. She had all but moved to Colombo, Sri Lanka, to help with the construction of a new mission, and a few weeks ago Greta received a disturbing e-mail that hinted of an impending marriage arranged by the leaders of the religion. Laurel had written to Greta to enlist her assistance in getting Milo to join her in Sri Lanka so that they could live as a big happy family. Though it was Milo who was detoxing when the e-mail arrived, it seemed to Greta that it was her sister whose head had been irretrievably altered.

Outside, Ilse shuffled past Greta and peeked into the unlocked front office. "Is there anyone here?" she called out. She was careful to keep both of her feet behind the entryway, as though a simple step would provoke a charge of trespassing. This fearfulness, so deeply ingrained in her parents, was something that Greta had combated (not altogether successfully) her entire life.

"I don't see why it should be closed," Greta said. "It's the middle of the day. Why don't we just take a look?" She headed toward a narrow dirt pathway running along the outside of the building. Enormous potted palm fronds flanked the trail, tipping toward each other to create an inviting tropical canopy. "Come on, Mama."

Ilse hesitated. Then, with a sigh, she hurried after her daughter. "I don't have much time, you know. We're going to have to be quick about this."

It was shaded and cool along the path, and for the first time since seeing her daughter that day, Ilse felt herself relax. Walking in Greta's slim gray shadow, she eyed the trees set in large terra-cotta containers and faintly shook her head. "Never much cared for palm trees."

"I know," Greta said. "I think maybe that's one of the reasons I don't like them." She realized even as she said it that it was an offering. *You see, Mother? We are alike in some way. Even though we disagree on everything, part of me will always be part of you.*

Ilse removed her glasses, breathed on the lenses, and wiped them with the tail of her faded red flannel shirt.

"Now, what is this garden you are doing, exactly? What happened to that lady you used? The one who charged you an arm and a leg?"

When Greta and Phillip were building their dream house, their architect had persuaded them to use a ridiculously overpriced landscaper, and for some reason Greta had made the mistake of telling her mother how much she had paid the woman. Ilse had never spent over a hundred dollars on a pair of shoes, and the extravagance that Greta had shown appalled her mother. Think of what could be done with that money! Who knew if that money would be there the rest of their lives? And what about Charlotte's college education? It was shameful. To make matters worse, the landscaper designed with ornamental grasses to match the house's modern aesthetic. Grass! Her daughter spent her husband's hard-earned money on *weeds*. If that landscaper knew anything at all, she would have known that pampas grass was a menace. She may as well have planted purple verbena or lantana. Of course, Ilse didn't say anything about it to Greta, but privately she railed against the development to her husband, Graham, surprising even herself by the tears of rage it provoked. Graham was perplexed, as he often was, by his wife's upset. Why should it matter so much to her? Newspapers had come to glean hard-earned knowledge from her, she spat. She couldn't count how many times people asked when she would go into business for herself. And her own daughter shut her out as though she was nothing but an amateur, some provincial farmer selling pickles at the county fair.

She asked after the designer now, not because she cared a bit about her but because it would be so lovely to hear Greta admit, for once, that it was a mistake.

"Oh . . ." Greta said vaguely, "I don't want to bother Lindsay with this. It's just something I'm doing on my own."

Annoyed, Ilse stamped her foot and felt something lodge itself in her shoe. Holding on to the edge of a container made of reclaimed wood, Ilse removed her shoe and shook out the offending pebble.

Greta lingered by a small white flower entwined on a trellis. "You know, I think 'cactuses' is correct, too. Like 'octopuses.' It just sounds wrong."

"Oh for heaven's sake," her mother muttered under her breath.

"What's this?" Greta took hold of a glossy leaf and rubbed it gently between her fingers.

"Stephanotis. Wedding flower," Ilse said, slipping her shoe back on. "Always tried to grow that one but never figured out a way to overwinter it. It would grow for you nicely in this climate."

Greta immediately released the flower and stepped away. The mention of the word "wedding" sickened her. It was four months now since she and Phillip had separated, four months since the revelation of his infidelity and deception and, inadvertently, the commencement of her own painful duplicity. Phillip had begged Greta to withhold the information from everyone until they made a definitive decision regarding their fate, and while Greta had agreed that this was best, the ache of concealment was all-consuming. Watching and judging her every sentence while at the same time studying to see if her duplicity managed to go undetected was an exhausting and insidious exercise. If she failed, she risked harming her daughter's sense of well-being and would be forced to make a decision she was not yet prepared to make. And if she succeeded, she had the dubious satisfaction of knowing that she could lie just as well as her husband, a quality for which she continued to malign him on a daily basis.

Her mother, whom she had tried without success to deceive as a teenager, took every lie now without question. Was it the distraction of Milo that kept her from questioning the signs? Phillip's protracted absences, the wedding pictures removed from the frames—even Charlotte noticed the missing pictures almost immediately. Scrambling to come up with a suitable lie, Greta told her daughter that they were ready for their annual cleaning; otherwise they wouldn't survive. Greta consoled herself that in a way what she was saying was true, if the photographs could be looked at as emblems of their marriage. Charlotte seemed to take this explanation willingly, even gratefully. Of course, Greta understood, she didn't want her world to end. Watching her skip away, believing the lie, was the bitterest triumph of all. At six years old, already her daughter was learning the art of deception as self-preservation. It was times such as these when Greta's hatred of the only man she had ever loved reached its zenith. An enmity so fierce and jagged she could almost feel it cutting her body from the inside, as if she had swallowed a handful of broken glass and the shards were struggling to work their way out.

She looked up just as Ilse disappeared around the bend. With the sounds of the ocean and the freeway on the one side and the camel-colored mountains on the other, Greta had the pleasant feeling of wandering down a secret garden path. So far they had encountered no one and Greta was increasingly unsure if she even wanted to. As the trees gave way to flowering shrub hedges and potted false cypresses, Greta found her mother staring at a vine with variegated heart-shaped leaves. Balancing on the stem, a peculiar brown flower resembled a small sea creature.

"What *is* that?" Greta asked. "It's amazing."

Ilse stared at the plant, frowning. She pressed her finger up to her forehead, as though the pressure would somehow retrieve the memory. She knew this plant—had even planted it and made cuttings of it for her friends—but now the name of it stubbornly eluded her.

"I don't know," she muttered.

"What do you mean you don't know?" Greta kneeled down and looked around for a label. "You know everything, Mama."

Ilse shook her head and walked on, defeated by her failing memory. Aging was an insult, any way you looked at it. It was God giving you the raspberry.

"Hang on!" Greta held up her phone and aimed it at the plant. "I'll Google it when I get home."

"Well, if you could do that, what do you need me for?"

When Greta caught up to her mother again, she was anxiously winding her old Timex watch. "What time do you have? I can't be late to the clinic."

"We have hours, Mama."

"Just want to make sure we aren't late, is all. Milo hasn't had anyone to depend on for most of his life. He needs to know that he can depend on me."

"And how is Dad with Milo moving in with you?"

Greta tried to sound casual, merely curious, but her mother bristled. "What do you mean, how is he with this? He's fine. He knows it's what we have to do."

Greta considered dropping it, but then she remembered her father's high blood pressure, the heart-attack scare years earlier, and all of the agonizing months they spent as he recuperated. The thought of her parents spending their twilight years taking in an addict who had done little to aid in his own recovery made her alternately frustrated and scared. Surely it could come to no good. It would only endanger the health of her father.

"Well . . . you don't really have to," Greta persevered. "There are places for kids like Milo. He could go to a halfway house.

Someplace where there are other kids who are struggling with the same issues—"

"So when he relapses, he'll have a buddy right there to do it with?" Ilse said. "No, thank you. We are family. This is what family does." She pointed to a hanging plant whose leaves resembled the horns of an animal. "Did you say this was a sun or shade garden?"

"I didn't say." It was clear to Greta that her mother was changing the subject. And if she had learned anything, she would be wise to just let it go. Her mother's mind was made up, and nothing—not Greta, not Greta's father's health, not even Ilse's own better judgment—would change her mind.

"Shade," Greta said, resigned. "Mostly shade, I guess."

They walked farther down the path, talking little, as Ilse pointed at the flora and commented and Greta dutifully took notes.

"Ficuses don't like to be moved. They will go in decline and die. . . . Spice bush has red flowers that smell like red wine. . . . Most people seem to think Sticky monkey-flowers require full shade, but it will flower for you more in partial shade. . . ."

It was pleasant for Ilse to watch Greta transcribe her words as if they mattered. Greta had been an assiduous student from the time she had entered the Presbyterian preschool. She would sit with pictureless books in her little lap before she even knew how to read, studying the writing as though all of the mystery and wonder of the world were contained in the strange indecipherable symbols. Her academic achievements were legion, and Ilse often found herself marveling at the natural depth of her daughter's intellect. Greta sailed through middle school and high school, and though she secured a full scholarship to the state school, Ilse and Graham scraped together whatever they could to send her to the Ivy League school of her choice.

Greta met Phillip her first year of Stanford, and although Ilse liked him, there was something about the relationship that galled her. Her daughter no longer seemed driven to succeed, preferring instead to rally behind Phillip's achievements.

Gradually it seemed not to matter to her at all—like the language of a country she no longer lived in. She ceased being at the top of her class in college, and her postgraduate career existed only until Phillip completed his MBA and started to earn a hefty salary. Then Greta set her sights on homemaking and, later, on mothering, with the same intensity that she had once possessed for her studies.

"Changing hydrangeas from pink to blue requires aluminum in the soil," Greta repeated, scribbling in her notebook. As her dark blond hair fell in her face, she tucked it behind her ear with her pencil. It was a gesture Ilse had seen her daughter make thousands of times, but Ilse noticed that there was something different about it. The change was almost indiscernible, and she set about trying to locate its origin. Greta's face had grown fuller in recent years, due to those fertility drugs she was taking Ilse supposed, but now her face was back to normal. In fact, it was a little gaunt. Had she stopped them? Could she be pregnant? Surely Greta would have told her . . . but then again, Greta had become more and more secretive over time. Ilse considered asking her daughter if she was pregnant, but she resented once again having to fish for information. Besides, upon closer examination, Greta wasn't pregnant. She just looked . . . worn. Greta, though never a great beauty, always seemed to have a light that illuminated her from the inside. And now, for the first time, it was dimmed.

"Are you eating enough?" Ilse blurted out.

Greta looked up, startled to see her mother's inscrutable gaze focused on her.

"Eating? Yes, I'm eating." She threw her notebook into her shoulder bag and wheeled around, turning her back to Ilse. For a moment, as she felt the adrenaline coursing through her veins, Greta made a quick conversational inventory in her mind, attempting to locate the misstep. Reviewing their short conversation, she decided that she had said nothing that would have raised suspicion. Her body had simply betrayed her. Quitting the fertility drugs upon discovering Phillip's affair, combined with her inability to keep almost anything down for what seemed like weeks, had made her skinnier than she had been in high school. And the lack of sleep from lying in bed at night trying not to imagine him mounting Theresa had given her eyes a haunted look. She had tried makeup to compensate for the dullness that had settled on her face like dust on a painting in a junk shop, but this only made it worse. Whatever beauty she thought she might have possessed she realized had only been through her husband's assessment of her. The shock of his infidelity was matched only by the pain of no longer seeing herself through his eyes. Now she saw herself as cruelly as he must have seen her.

How foolish Greta had been to think that she could have

held him in her thrall, that he would be immune to beauty. The object of his desire had been as fluid as molten glass—not yet formed, ready to bend to his will. Theresa was truly something blooming. Greta could see that, and yet somehow stupidly she never once considered the possibility. She wanted him, he told Greta in one of the most raggedly honest moments of their marriage, during the brief pause before she closed her heart to him. The girl wanted him and that had been enough. A man who had only just begun to suspect that he would never rise above the ordinary. It would have taken a god not to heed the siren's call.

Ocean mist traveled over the tops of the trees and shrubs and enshrouded the limbs of the two silently advancing women. Ilse was curious as to how long the path would go on, and even though walking had become more difficult these past couple of years, she forged ahead. Greta trailed behind her, moody and restless. The sunlight that filtered through the trees cast a light that looked to Ilse like needle lace, the kind her mother had specialized in. If she hadn't been caught up in the memory of this, the boy wouldn't have taken her by surprise.

"Oh!" Ilse cried out, staggering backward. She reached out to the trunk of a coral-barked maple for balance.

A faded tattoo of an ornate crucifix covered one side of the boy's neck, and both arms were covered with other religious imagery and Spanish writing. He was bending down, tinkering with the plastic tubing from an automatic watering system.

When he stood, he seemed as surprised to see Ilse as she was to see him. He jutted out his chin slightly in a quick gesture of recognition and then crouched down again.

Greta rushed forward to help her mother, but Ilse just brushed her away with embarrassment. "*Hola,*" Greta said to the boy, demonstrating the extent of her Spanish.

"Hello, Missus," the boy said in accented English. "Is closed today. Tomorrow is open." He smiled, and his teeth shone against his brown skin. He was a beautiful young man, in his late teens or early twenties, Greta guessed. It might have been the proximity of age, or the strong healthy air of the boy that caused Ilse to hurry back in the direction from which they had come.

"Wait!" Greta called after her.

But Ilse didn't slow down. Greta hurried to catch up to her. When she did, she grabbed her by the elbow, and her mother instinctively jerked her arm away.

"What are you doing?"

Ilse kept walking. "I don't want to be late picking up Milo. I told you that."

"And I told you that you won't be."

"You don't know that. I'd rather get there early and wait than—"

"Than spend any more time with me than you have to?"

Ilse glanced at Greta with a withering expression of annoyance. Greta had seen it many times over the years when she resorted to sarcasm.

"I came here for Milo," Ilse said. "I want to get him home safely. I want to take him home before he changes his mind."

"And what makes you think that he won't change his mind when you get him there? You're just going to bring a heroin addict into your house? How are you going to feel when you wake up in the morning and find everything of value gone? Your jewelry? Or Dad's models. Think about that, Mama. He shoots heroin, and has since he was fifteen—"

"He wants to stop," Ilse said, her voice rising.

"Yeah, what he wants and what he's capable of are two different things."

Ilse raised her hands to the side of her face. "What can I do, Greta? Milo is my grandson. My only grandson. You expect me to lie down and not do everything in my power to save him?" She shook her head. "I don't expect you to understand this."

"He isn't Rory," Greta said.

"God forbid you will ever think to yourself there was something that you could have done to save someone that you love. God forbid you should ever have to lie awake at night, playing it over and over again in your mind. What if I had called him that night? Rory would have come if I asked him. What if . . ." She stopped herself and closed her eyes. She reached her hand across to the nearest tree to steady herself. Pain, regret, and guilt mingled just under the surface, the aggregate of all her profound sadness.

"He isn't Rory," Greta repeated softly.

"I know," Ilse said, her voice tinged with anguish. "But I see so much of Rory in him. He's lost, Greta. He needs me."

"He needs his *mother*," Greta said.

Ilse flicked her hand, brushing away the unpleasant thought as if it were a cobweb. "And who is going to bring Laurel back? You? Please . . . your sister has made her choice," she added bitterly.

They walked on, retracing their steps through the mist.

"I just don't want you and Dad to be disappointed," Greta said. "You raised your kids—you ought to be enjoying life now."

"You never stop raising your kids, Greta. And your kids' kids. Maybe some people can go on and wash their hands, but I can't."

"Mama, he stole from you. He took money from you and Dad and went out and bought drugs with it. You are inviting danger into your home."

"And what about second chances, Greta?"

Second chances. Greta tried to envision her own six-year-old daughter desperate and addicted. It was nearly impossible to imagine, but even in the hypothetical, it was clear that the chances Greta would give her were endless. Phillip had betrayed her, but unlike her daughter, the thought of giving him a second chance was agonizing to consider. Would it have been different if he had betrayed her in another way? Gambled the house away? If she had discovered that he was an addict?

But even as Greta considered the limits of her own tenuous capacity to forgive, she knew that it wasn't really Milo to whom her mother was giving a second chance. That was clear. By saving Milo from himself, she was attempting to right the past. She was reaching her hands into the wreckage of the car that Saturday night and carrying her son away with her alive. It was a chimera her mother was chasing, Greta knew, but she also knew that it was no use trying to hold her back. Her mother would die trying.

As they neared the exit, the mist had begun to dissipate. Sunshine was burrowing through gaps in the bushes and trees. Ilse pointed to a small tree with a dark brown trunk and heart-shaped leaves.

"Do you remember when you were little, you dragged one of these all the way home from the bus stop? Someone left it by the trash, and you insisted that we plant it in the garden. You took it on yourself to rehabilitate it. You stripped the quilt from your bed and wrapped it around the trunk." Ilse smiled. "You remember that?"

Greta stared at the tree, searching her memory. "I think so. . . . But are you sure it wasn't Laurel?"

"Laurel never had any interest in the garden. It was you."

Greta tried to connect the memory of the girl who nursed a dying abandoned tree to the woman she was now.

"It was a redbud," Ilse said. "Like this one."

"Mama?"

Ilse turned and looked at Greta. "What?"

Suddenly the urge to confess was overwhelming. Greta placed her open palm against her own mouth to stop herself. *Phillip betrayed me. My marriage has been over for almost half a year, and I don't know how to tell my daughter. I don't know what to do with my life. I'm so scared.* But something in her mother's expression arrested her. Perhaps it was the worry etched in her forehead or the frailty that had manifested itself in the gentle but marked curvature of her spine. As she stood in the returning sunlight, looking down into the pale blue of her mother's eyes, Greta felt the strange and heretofore unfamiliar sensation of something being lifted from her—a weight that only later she was able to identify as her childhood.

"What?" Ilse asked again. "What is it?"

"Let's go get Milo," Greta said. "He's waiting for you."

MY OLIVIA

OLIVER WAS JUST SHY OF four years old when he asked his
mother to buy him a dress for the first time. It was a simple red
shift, almost a tunic, with a band of metallic rickrack just above
the hem, but something in the color or the cut or the way that
it was modeled on the fiberglass child-size mannequin in the
boutique window made it unmistakably a dress.

Oliver was Marina's only child, the result of an impetuous
island holiday she had taken with girlfriends in order to lift her
spirits after yet another failed relationship. She had never been
to the Caribbean, and her girlfriends Merle, Trudie, and Una
pooled their funds to splurge for a suite right on the water. It
was a raucous, rum-soaked weekend full of girlish tear-stained
confessions and ninety-minute massages in the height of hur-
ricane season. When Marina returned to California with stuffy
sinuses and a sudden dislike for the smell of coffee, she was sure
that she had contracted a bug.

Being in her late thirties and never having had anything close to a pregnancy scare, Marina had always assumed that she was simply infertile. But unlike her friends, who went from fearing pregnancy to pursuing it, Marina viewed her situation as a convenience or even a luxury since she had never once heard the ticking of her own clock. She assumed that the clock was broken along with her reproductive machinery and didn't concern herself much with it. The inability to sustain a relationship with a man was far more worrisome.

It was Trudie who first suggested to Marina that she might be pregnant, after Marina ran to the bathroom twice while watching Trudie feed her baby pureed leftover spaghetti and meatballs with a spoon. It had been just over three months since the Barbados holiday.

"It isn't possible," Marina insisted. "I got my period."

"You might want to get a test, just in case," Trudie told her in a singsong voice. "Zachariah was a surprise. Weren't you, my little Zach pack!" She kissed her boy extravagantly on the mouth and licked the sauce from the sides of her own lips, sending Marina sprinting to the toilet again. That night she picked up a pregnancy test kit on the way home from the gym and was stunned to see the plus sign materialize. She stared at the contraption in disbelief, doubting its accuracy. When the blue cross appeared on the second test, even more rapidly this time, she sat down on the edge of the bathtub, shaking her head. Holding the innocuous-looking piece of plastic in her hand, she was transfixed by the bright blue stain in its tiny window. It was like she had found a bruise that had appeared on her body overnight, with no knowledge of how or when the injury had taken place.

What Marina had assumed to be her menstruation was actually implantation bleeding; the cluster of cells that would later become her son was burrowing into her uterine wall. By the time she discovered the pregnancy, she was already well into her second trimester. Marina was dumbfounded. The thought of becoming a mother was unfathomable to her. She had only ever been vaguely interested in her friends' children, a notable source of contention with her last serious boyfriend. One of their recurring arguments had been her patent lack of interest in having a family.

"There's something wrong with you," he insisted. "You have the maternal instincts of a black widow."

"Black widows eat their mates, not their young," she replied. It was a useless correction, however; she could tell by the sad smile and the way that the corners of his eyes tilted down that it was already over between them. And it was true, Marina had no interest in motherhood. She relished her freedom with a zeal that only grew stronger as she watched her girlfriends' steady marches toward maternity. One by one, their personalities became as disfigured as their bodies. They were perpetually fatigued and unkempt, their walls were covered with sloppy finger paintings housed in expensive frames, and their speech was taken over by motherese—peppered with the words "potty," "wee-wee," and "wa-wa." One night, Una actually

licked her finger and rubbed it across Marina's cheek, only realizing her gaffe when she saw the dumbstruck expression on
her childless friend's face.

"Oh! Sorry, honey." Una laughed. "Mommy's got baby
brain!"

Marina wanted no part of it. As soon as she escaped the
mommy brigade, it took twenty minutes on the elliptical until
she began to feel like herself again.

And then for five long months, she watched her body meta-
morphose into exactly what she disparaged in her friends. The
years that she had spent perfecting those twin lines down the
sides of her abdomen, the delicate sloping inside toward her
navel—she would have to say good-bye to these forever. At
night, if she was really quiet, she felt as if she could hear the
muscles tearing.

Marina followed her obstetrician's advice and ate the mini-
mum amount required to sustain the life of what she viewed as
the alien growing inside of her, but even with that, there was
no stopping the ruthless expansion; once she hit the thirty-
pound mark over her ideal weight, she stopped stepping on the
metal-and-glass bathroom scale. She grew deeply depressed
when she could no longer wear her own clothes, and yet refused to buy anything that she wouldn't need again, thinking
it wasteful. Her friends donated boxes of frumpy, drool-stained
maternity clothes to her, which she thanked them for as she
resigned herself to the ugly garments. Gritting her teeth, she
avoided her own reflection and waited and waited and waited
for the reprieve.

And then, exactly on the due date, Marina woke up with contractions. Three hours later she was holding her seven-and-a-half-pound son in her arms, staring in awe as he snuffled around her breast and fastened on with a hungry little rosebud mouth. She had never seen a face so fine and symmetrical in her life. He didn't look anything like her, but very much like the caramel-skinned surf instructor she had rolled around on the beach with during those last nights of her holiday. Her baby had a soft carpet of circles covering his tiny head, and gray eyes the color of pussywillows. He was the most beautiful creature she had ever laid eyes on, and Marina was shocked to find herself at the age of thirty-seven so deeply in love. She named him Oliver.

For the first few weeks, Marina was terrified that she would not be able to keep Oliver alive. Never had she had even so much as a plant to take care of, let alone a little boy. Growing up, her family had an outdoor dog, but mostly her father took care of it. Marina personally never had anything to do with the dog, and if her parents went away on vacation, they would hire a dog walker to come by each day, feed the animal, and give it a modicum of affection. This was so that they wouldn't return to a situation, as they did the first time they had left Marina home alone, where the dog nearly starved.

When Oliver was a baby, Marina found herself waking up in the middle of the night terrified that he had stopped breathing. She stripped his crib of any potential smothering hazards, getting rid of stuffed animals, pillows, bumpers, and blankets, but even with this precaution in place, Marina would find herself in his room night after night, camped out next to his crib, listening for the sweet inhalation and exhalation of his tiny lungs.

And despite or perhaps because of her fears, Oliver thrived. Though not particularly hefty, he hit all of his developmental milestones and was thought to be an exceedingly healthy child. He was breastfed longer than most children and never exhibited anything resembling an allergy: peanuts, shellfish, soy, dust, dander . . . nothing threatened him. The only thing to which he demonstrated an adverse reaction was a haircut. Oliver screamed anytime a pair of scissors came close to his long, curly hair. The first two words he uttered in sequence occurred when Marina brought him to a children's hair salon for his first haircut.

"NO, MOMMY!" He held out his arms to her, his gray eyes widened in terror. The experienced stylist tried to distract him with cartoons and, when that didn't work, to bribe him with lollipops and Hershey's Kisses, but Oliver continued to howl in protest. When it was clear that Oliver would not submit, Marina scooped him up and paid the woman anyway, overtipping as she mumbled an embarrassed apology and rushed out of the salon.

Now, at six years old, Oliver had dark, curly, shoulder-length hair. Marina mastered the French braid so that she could fake a short haircut when necessary, but most of the time Oliver wore his hair loose in soft glossy waves that arranged themselves around his delicate face. He was beautiful, but more than that, he was pretty. Marina was used to people asking her the name of her little girl. "*His* name is Oliver," she would say. "He's a boy," she would add, and smile at the ill-disguised looks of disbelief.

She wasn't exactly sure when Oliver became Olivia at home. Most of the time she called him Oll, or Ollie, but just after his fourth birthday—shyly at first and then with more insistence—he asked that she call him Olivia.

"But Oliver honey, you're a boy."

"I want to tell you a secret," he said.

They were snuggled in her bed reading *Raggedy Ann in the Deep Deep Woods*. She put the book aside and looked down at him.

"Okay, honey. What's the secret?"

"Well . . ." He looked nervous, and then grinned at her. "I wasn't going to tell you, but you're my mommy."

"That's right, hon. I'm your mommy, and you can tell me anything. Anything at all."

"I'm really a girl," he said in a whisper.

She stared at him, wanting to say the right thing, fearing to say the wrong thing.

"You may *feel* like a girl sometimes . . ." she began.

"No! I *am* a girl," he said, his voice rising.

She waited a moment for him to calm down and then, gently, she tried again to explain. "Do you remember when we had that talk how what you have between your legs is different than what mommy has and—"

"My penis is going to fall off," he said. "And when it does, everyone will know that I'm not lying. I'm a girl. My name is Olivia!" He put his head down in her lap and cried. She ran her hands through the tangle of his hair and did the only thing that she knew how to do. She comforted him.

Marina sat in the shade of a silver maple tree next to the father of Oliver's best friend while they watched their respective off-spring swing from the monkey bars. Though it was April in Southern California, the promise of spring seemed to have become the unseasonably punishing heat of summer. Marina hid beneath her sunhat while her friend sat beside her, exposed, getting redder and redder.

"Don't tell me you aren't wearing sunscreen," she said to him.

Phillip fanned himself with the sheaf of papers in his hand.

"I'm a man," he said.

"You're an idiot," she said, grinning, and punched him in the arm. She opened her bag and took out a packet of moistened sunscreen wipes.

"You aren't going to put that on me, are you?"

"Are you kidding?" she said. "These things are expensive! I don't like you that much. Charlotte!"

She yelled at the blond girl dangling from the monkey bars behind her son. "Ollie, honey. You and Charlotte come here!"

The kids dropped to the soft dirt and raced over to their parents.

"Feel how hot I am," Charlotte said as she climbed up on Phillip's lap and touched her cheek to his.

"You are hot," he said. "And Daddy wasn't thinking when he didn't put any sunscreen on you this morning. . . ."

"Mama always puts sunscreen on me," Charlotte said.

"I'm sure she does." Phillip took a deep breath and let the air out slowly.

"Here, let me help . . ." Marina reached out and swiped the towelette across Charlotte's face, neck, and bare arms.

"I don't need sunscreen!" Oliver crowed. "I don't get sunburned 'cause I have dark skin already!"

"Not so fast," Marina took another towelette and performed the same task on her son. "Skin cancer is for everyone," she said, handing the used towelettes to her son. "Go throw these away, and then you can do more monkey bars."

The children scampered off, screaming something unintelligible.

"Thanks," Phillip said. "And the neglectful parent of the year award goes to . . ."

"Whatever. You owe me a Coke."

Phillip smiled at her and then glanced down at his Black-Berry.

"Sorry, I have to put this fire out."

"Go ahead," Marina said.

She took off her hat and wiped away the perspiration from her forehead, then put her hat back on. It had been several months now since she and Phillip had begun meeting for a standing playdate, usually every other weekend when it was Phillip's turn with his daughter. Phillip and Charlotte's mother had separated some time after the holidays, and though Charlotte seemed to be taking the situation in stride, Phillip carried the air of a man condemned. Not wanting to pry, Marina didn't ask for the specifics of his marital difficulties, but she surmised from his guilty countenance that he was in some way responsible—while knowing enough about relationships to acknowledge that their failure was rarely, if ever, unilateral. They all have a built-in expiration date, Marina thought, and if people would just realize this up front they could save themselves a lot of pain. Why not just appreciate the time they have together—the exalted sex, the precious antecedent moments of rapture, the delight of finding the sublime in the banal? Instead, we demand that the other hold up a mirror and reflect back to us everything we hope to believe about ourselves. And we love them for it . . . until the mirror becomes too heavy to hold, or breaks altogether, and then the punishment never ceases. But, ah, this was coming from Marina. She had not had even one sustained relationship since her son's birth, and strikingly few before. For years she had more or less resigned herself to a life alone, but then recently she found herself drawn to the sad and guilty man beside her.

Phillip bobbed his knee up and down while he listened with mounting impatience to the caller.

"Uh-huh. Uh-huh." He nudged Marina with the tip of his foot and mouthed the words "*I'm sorry.*" She waved her hand at him and deliberately turned to watch the kids playing in the distance to give him space. The children had taken a break from the monkey bars and now sat facing each other, their legs in a V, toes touching, talking. She could tell that Oliver was telling a story, and she tried to decipher its subject from the grand hand gestures. Charlotte threw her head back and the high tinkling laughter traveled all the way to the bench where their parents sat.

"God, it's nice to hear her laugh," Phillip said. He had finished the phone call and slipped his BlackBerry into the breast pocket of his broadcloth button-down.

"I think Ollie could make anyone laugh. He could make the Taliban laugh," she said.

Phillip smiled and ran a hand through his closely cropped blond hair. "Christ, it's hot. I'd like to round up all those global-warming naysayers shoulder to shoulder and just watch them bake."

Marina laughed. "Well, that would be my entire family."

Phillip raised an eyebrow with interest. "No kidding."

"Yup. No such thing as global warming. Evolution is questionable. And, of course, homosexuals are all going to hell."

"And where exactly did you come from?" Phillip asked.

"Orange County," she said. "From the virginal loins of Joyce Pennock née Hartcourt. I think my parents did it precisely three times in their lives, and each time she got knocked up."

"Brothers? Sisters?" Phillip asked.

"One of each," Marina said. "And boy-oh-boy do they toe the party line. Ollie and I are the black sheep of the family. Literally." She laced her fingers above her head and stretched. She noticed his eyes flit across her ribcage and then just as quickly dart away. "Holidays are loads of fun at the Pennocks'."

"All families are horrible, aren't they?" Phillip said. "I mean, I don't think I've ever met anyone who just straight-out likes their family."

"That's depressing," Marina said.

"I shouldn't say that. I mean, mine really wasn't so bad."

She was about to ask for details when he took the vibrating phone out of his pocket and looked at it. She glanced over at the screen and saw the face of Charlotte's mother.

"Go ahead," she told him.

Phillip jumped up and walked a few feet away from their bench. Marina had only met Phillip's estranged wife once in passing at their children's school, when they found themselves standing alone in the school parking lot several minutes too early for pickup. Marina introduced herself as the mother of Oliver, Charlotte's friend. The woman nodded and smiled, but Marina had the strange feeling that she was looking through her, as though Marina were invisible. They exchanged e-mail addresses and the vague promise of setting up a playdate. This was at the beginning of the school year. Marina sent her two e-mails that remained unanswered. A few months later she and Phillip got to know each other, and she was relieved that a friendship with her was never forged.

Marina watched Phillip pace while he talked on the phone. His back curved suddenly as though a weight had been placed on his shoulders, pitching him forward. With the phone up to his ear and his other hand wrapped around his forehead, he pressed his thumb and index finger into the pressure points of his temples. "He's a disaster," Marina thought. "Toxic," she could hear Una say. "Unavailable," said Merle. "Damaged," said Trudie. As her gaggle of married girlfriends listed the litany of his many obvious failings, Marina knew that given the chance, she would surely go to bed with him anyway.

"Okay, okay! I hear what you're saying. And I'm sorry," she heard Phillip say. He walked back to the bench and began gathering Charlotte's things. "I'm just in the park with her now. I can meet you in a half hour." Phillip's face was red. "If we hurry, maybe fifteen, okay? I'm sorry. I . . ." He stood for a moment with the phone in his hand. It was clear to Marina that she had hung up.

"Everything okay?" she asked him, knowing it wasn't.

He grabbed Charlotte's tote and his messenger bag.

"I'm sorry. I—"

"Hey. You don't need to say you're sorry to me."

"It's a habit," he said.

She reached out and grabbed his wrist. She could feel his pulse race against her fingers.

"Well, you need to stop it," she said, still holding on to him.

Phillip looked at her, clearly surprised by the touch. He snapped his head around—to find his daughter, she figured—and she dropped his hand, embarrassed by her forwardness.

"Let me be the person you don't apologize to. That's all I mean."

Phillip reached out and turned up the brim of her sunhat. She looked straight into his eyes. She had never seen that color on a man. They reminded her of an old Edwardian ring that she had inherited from her grandmother—what was the stone? Tourmaline? Aquamarine? She noticed a birthmark next to his left eye and wanted to kiss it.

"Thank you," he said.

When he turned away from her, she felt herself exhale, not realizing that she had been holding her breath.

"Where are they?" Phillip said.

Hearing the panic in his voice, she ran toward the playground, scanning the monkey bars and jungle gyms.

"Ollie!" she screamed. Frightened children looked up at her. She could feel her heart beating wildly and her stomach drop as though she were descending in the elevator in a skyscraper. Several kids scattered, running into the protective embraces of their multicultural nannies. She saw Phillip sprint in the direction of the stone bathroom fixtures on the other side of the playground, along the edge of the parking lot. Just as he reached the building, she saw the two kids run out, holding hands, with their fingers interlaced.

Even from a distance, Marina could tell that the children had swapped clothing. Charlotte wore the gender-nonspecific tunic that she had purchased for Oliver in a store specializing in beachwear, while Oliver was dressed in Charlotte's floral sundress and her pink patent-leather sandals, his hair unbraided and bunched into two ponytails. By the time Marina reached the children, Charlotte was crying, frightened by Phillip's anger. He was on his knees holding her while she whimpered.

Marina looked down at her son, who watched the father and daughter with an uncertain expression.

"Ollie . . ."

"We wanted to play opposites," he told his mother quietly. "It's opposite day."

"It's okay, honey," she said, running her hand up and down his neck.

"It's *not* okay," Phillip said. "You don't just run off without telling anyone."

In Phillip's eyes she imagined that she could see the flicker of blame.

"He's right, Ollie," Marina said. "You both scared us."

Charlotte kept her head buried in her father's shoulder. "It was Ollie's idea," she heard her say in between sobs.

Oliver grabbed on to his mother's leg, blinking back tears himself. "It's opposite day!" he said again.

Marina remembered the things that they had left on the park bench. "Hey," she said to Phillip, "Do you want me to take them into the bathroom and change them, and I'll meet you at your car?"

Phillip stood up, carrying Charlotte in his arms.

"Can we just do the exchange later? She'll kill me if I'm not there in the next few minutes."

Charlotte popped her head up. "Who's going to kill you, Daddy?"

"No one," he said. He ran off in the direction of the car. Marina took her son's hand, and together they walked back to the bench in rare silence.

"Are you sure he was blaming you? Did he actually *say* it was your fault?"

Marina perched on the kitchen island in Trudie's restored

Craftsman and watched her friend assemble a complicated pasta dish. Oliver played a game on Marina's iPhone while lying on the living room couch; Trudie's two girls were already asleep in their bedroom.

"No," Marina said. "He didn't say it was my fault. He didn't say it was anyone's fault. But it was the way he looked at . . ." Marina didn't say Oliver's name, but she pointed in the direction of the living room.

Trudie nodded. "Well, anytime kids take off their clothes . . ." She didn't finish her sentence.

Marina chewed on an olive and spit the pit in an ashtray with the words THANK YOU FOR NOT SMOKING written on it.

"Please, Trudie. They're six years old. What are they going to see?" She grabbed another olive. "And I think we all know that Ollie is not interested in Charlotte's body. He wanted her clothes. He wanted the sundress with the flowers on it and the pink sandals. There's no desire there. Or if there is desire, it's the desire to look like her."

Trudie poured the pasta into a baking dish and refilled Marina's glass.

"Have you thought of taking him somewhere?" Trudie asked. "Like a therapist or something?"

"To do what? What's a therapist going to do? No one is going to convince him that he's a boy. And I can't *make* him a girl. He already resents me for it. It's like he thinks it's my fault that I gave birth to him and made him a boy."

She craned her head around to see if Oliver was eavesdropping. He seemed entirely absorbed in his game.

"I don't know what to do with him." She shook her head and drank deeply from her wineglass. "I really don't."

Trudie set the timer on the oven and poured herself a glass of pinot noir.

"I wouldn't discount therapy. You know Ellie was seeing someone."

"No, I didn't know that," Marina said. "Why?"

"Night terrors. She'd always been a perfect sleeper. We 'Ferberized' her just like we did Alice, and then out of the blue she started screaming at night. Sometimes two or three times a night."

"Jesus!" Marina said. "I had no idea."

Trudie shrugged. "Ron doesn't want me to talk about it. I tell him it's silly, I mean it's the twenty-first century. Therapy is hardly taboo. But he says he doesn't want to 'pathologize' our child."

"Sure, sure," Marina said. "I can understand that." She didn't understand. But then again, she didn't really understand what her friend even saw in her husband. Ron was a drip, Marina thought. But unlike most drips who at least manage to be innocuous in their drippiness, Ron asserted himself by thrusting his opinions on his gentle and conflict-avoidant wife.

"It's been months now, and Ellie's sleeping through the night just fine again. Personally I think she was a miracle worker. I was at the end of my rope."

"Mommy?" Marina looked over at Oliver who stood in the doorway holding her cell phone out to her. "Charlotte's daddy is on the phone. He wants to talk to you."

The smell of early blooming jasmine and honeysuckle lingered in the air as Marina sat on her porch with her laptop, distracting herself with work while she waited for Phillip. He had asked to see her, and she had told him to stop by after she put Oliver to bed. Picking up on her nervous energy, her son dragged out his bedtime even more than usual, begging for more pages to be read, more water to drink, and more trips to the bathroom after lights-out. Marina surreptitiously texted Phillip three times asking him to come later. After the last time, when he didn't reply for ten minutes, she was afraid that he would cancel and found herself unjustly furious with her son.

"Are you still mad at me, Mommy?" he asked. "I won't do it again."

Marina took a deep breath and grabbed him in a tight embrace. "No, my love. I'm not mad. I just have work that I need to get to, that's all." She felt guilty for omitting the fact that she was expecting Phillip, but until she knew what the visit was about, she wasn't comfortable mentioning it. Oliver was extremely possessive, never having had to share Marina with anyone. She hadn't even spent the night with anyone since before he was born.

Perched on the teak bench, she tried to concentrate on the catalog layout she was designing. A small soy-candle company had hired Marina to glamorize its image—to take it out of the crunchy patchouli-scented air of its origins and into something trendier and upmarket; but frustratingly the company kept asking her to go back and change the layouts every time she tried anything new. She was resizing the candles against different-colored backgrounds and fussing with the fonts when Phillip's Volvo pulled up.

"Hey," he said as he walked toward her. He carried a six-pack of Heineken in his hand.

Marina's heart leaped into her throat, and all of the boldness and brashness that she relied upon with most everyone deserted her.

"Hi, hi," she said shyly. "I didn't know this was bring-your-own-beer." She snapped her laptop shut and tucked it under her arm. Phillip leaned back against a post and looked down at her through eyes half-closed.

"Long day," he said.

"Yeah." She wasn't sure if he was referring to his day or hers. She got up and took the six-pack from him. He seemed taller than she remembered, though most of the time they spent together they were seated in a playground. "Let me open one of these for you," she said. "Unless you want to do it with your teeth and impress me."

"Oh, I would hope I could find other ways to impress you," he said with a smile.

Marina turned away from him and headed into the house. His comment set her mind into a flurry of interpretation. *What did it mean? Did he mean . . . Was he just bantering? Are we flirting?* She could feel her pulse quickening, and as much as she wanted to be near him, there was something about the proximity that felt sudden and painful. Like sticking your toes in ice-cold water before submerging yourself entirely. There is always that deliciously uncomfortable bit you need to get through.

When she returned to the porch, Phillip was sitting on the bench. She handed him the beer and a glass and sat cross-legged beside him with a mug of peppermint tea.

"You probably don't want the glass," she said.

"Straight-from-the-bottle kind of guy," he said. He took a swig and leaned back against the wall of the house. "It's nice to hang out at night for once."

"Yeah, we're really branching out," Marina said. "Sitting on a completely different bench."

Phillip laughed. He looked at her sideways. "I like your hair like that. It's funny, I always thought I would marry a redhead."

Marina touched her hair, piled up on top of her head and casually fastened with a pin.

"I'm sorry I had to keep postponing," Marina said. "It's like Ollie has this sixth sense . . ."

"I'm the one who wanted to apologize," Phillip said, sitting forward and touching her knee. "I was a jerk today, when the kids—"

"Oh, that," she said. "I figured you were just stressed about your . . ."

"Wife. She's still my wife," he said slowly, as if he was telling himself as much as her.

"Right. Okay. I didn't know what was going on with that. . . ."

She felt a shock of embarrassment, suddenly realizing that perhaps this attraction she felt was entirely one-sided. "Well, apology accepted," she said, trying to sound bright and carefree. "I know it's late and if you need to—"

"Marina, I really like you," he interrupted. "A lot. Probably too much, considering that I'm a mess right now."

"It's okay," she said, feeling somehow both relieved and anxious at the same time. "Listen, you don't have to explain anything. I know. I mean, I *don't* know, but I can just imagine how messy these things are."

"I fucked up," he said. "I fucked up in the most monumental, bastardly way."

"Is that even a word, 'bastardly'?" she said.

He ignored her and continued. It almost seemed like a recitation.

"I hurt, my wife . . . I hurt . . . well, let's just say that I have hurt and disappointed every woman that I have come into contact with—and I'm including my daughter in this—and I don't want to do it anymore. I can't do it anymore."

Marina nodded and blew on her tea before taking a sip.

"I'm a big girl," she said. "Well, actually I'm a size four, but . . ."

"Do you understand what I'm saying?" He looked at her without a trace of irony. "I think it's the *not* talking that got me into this shit mess I'm in now. And I *like* talking to you. I don't want to lose that."

Marina felt dull with the loss of intrigue. He was being honest with her, and in her experience that usually didn't come until months, even years, later, if ever. Her body suddenly felt cold even while her face seemed to burn with embarrassment.

"I get that," she said. "And thanks. You're a good guy. Don't let anyone tell you different."

Phillip shook his head and she could see the sneer of self-loathing on his face. "Enough about me," he said.

"Hey, I have Charlotte's dress," she said. "And her shoes. Don't let me forget to give those to you."

"So . . . what is going on there anyway? I've been meaning to ask you."

"What do you mean?"

He shifted position on the bench. She could tell that he was searching for a way to broach the obvious.

"With Oliver. The, uh, switching clothes. Is this something . . . new?" he asked.

"No, I'd say this has been happening for a long time."

"And what does his father say about it? If it's too personal, just tell me to shut up."

"His father doesn't know. Or, more precisely, he doesn't know that Oliver exists." Marina drew her legs out from under her. They had fallen asleep, and she stomped her feet lightly on the wooden floor of the porch to wake them. "I met him when I was on vacation. He was a surf instructor. I only saw him for the weekend. Gorgeous man. Oliver looks exactly like him."

"Why didn't you ever tell him that he has a son?"

She sipped her tea. It had gone from hot to cold with strange swiftness.

"I almost did. When I was about eight months pregnant, I

had the brilliant idea to call him. He had given me his number, and it seemed like the decent thing to do. I was pretty sure that he wouldn't be interested in moving to the States, but I thought, someone's having your kid, you never know. . . ."

Phillip set his empty beer bottle on the floor next to him.

"You want another?" she asked him

"Later," he said. "Go on."

"So I called the number, and this little girl answers the phone. With a high squeaky voice, and that accent? I should have just hung up right then. But like an idiot, I wasn't thinking it through. 'May I speak to James?' I ask. The girl tells me that her father isn't there, and she puts her mother on the phone."

"Oh Jesus," Phillip said.

"Yeah. I don't know why, but I don't hang up. And then this woman tells me that her name is Tamsin and asks me why I want to talk to her husband."

"What did you say?"

Marina pulled up her legs and wrapped her arms around her knees.

"I said . . . I said that he was my teacher a few months ago and that I wanted to thank him." Marina laughed and shook her head. "It was the only thing I could think of. So she asked me my name, and I told her."

"You gave her your real name?" Phillip asked

"Yep. 'Well, Marina, I will tell him,' she says. 'But he has many students, so I doubt he will remember you.' I thanked her, and just before I hung up, I asked her how many kids she had. Three. He had three little girls."

They were quiet for a moment and listened to a car alarm sounding in the distance. Phillip cleared his throat. "What are you going to do about the, uh, what do you call it? The wanting to be a girl? Is this okay to talk about? I don't want to if . . ."

"No," Marina said. "God no. I *want* to talk about it. I don't know what to do. He *is* a girl."

"Well, right now he wants to be a girl, that's clear," Phillip said. "But who knows how he's going to feel later?"

"Yeah, I guess," she replied, unconvinced. "Honestly, though, I'm pretty certain this is here to stay. It's just who he is. I feel like people look at me like I'm encouraging it, or somehow I'm *making* him this way. Do you know how many stupid boys' things I've bought him? How many cars and trucks and airplanes? The footballs and baseball bats? This isn't even counting the crap that my family buys him. I've told them to stop wasting their money, but every birthday and Christmas, Ollie gets a big ol' testosterone-laden present."

Phillip laughed. "What do you do with them?"

"He throws them away," she said. "Or he hides them."

She and Phillip lingered on the porch together for another hour. They talked about her son, her failed relationships, his daughter, his wife, his former mistress, his job, and all of the mistakes they had made and if not vowed then at least hoped never to repeat. And before parting, against their better judgment, they shared a lonely kiss that they both knew, as soon as it was over, would be added to the long list of regrets.

———————

The next Sunday morning Marina and Oliver went to the park alone. It was Charlotte's weekend with her mother, and Phillip told Marina that he would be in Chicago on an extended business trip. Marina halfheartedly attempted to scare up a playdate for her son, but this day, like so many others before it, all of his classmates were otherwise engaged. She tried not to think that it was related to Oliver's increasing insistence on passing as a girl—after all, she had specifically sought out the most progressive school possible, in a city more tolerant than most. Regardless, it seemed that the older Oliver became, the less he was invited to playdates. When Marina asked his teacher, a thirty-five-year primary-school veteran, whether Oliver was being shunned by his classmates, Mercedes reassured Marina that he had plenty of friends, boys as well as girls. She then proceeded to detail the school's mission of tolerance and diversity—a lecture that Marina had heard many times before and no longer found reassuring.

"But why doesn't anyone call us for playdates?" Marina asked. "It's like they think that he has a disease and they're afraid their kid is going to catch it."

Mercedes clicked her tongue and insisted that there was only acceptance from his classmates. Before Marina left, however, Mercedes delicately broached the idea of Marina taking Oliver to see a "gender specialist" referred by the school counselor.

At the park, Oliver rode his purple bike beside Marina. The weather had cooled considerably, and as a compromise to Marina's insistence that he wear a hoodie over his favorite pink-striped "Wonder Bunny" T-shirt and leggings underneath his shorts, Oliver was allowed to borrow one of Marina's scarfs. He tied the long flowing scarf around his waist, knotting it on the side to lie over his shorts as a makeshift skirt.

Zipping along on his bicycle, he circled back to Marina for a third time, nudging her forward like a sheepdog. "You don't have to wait for me, honey," she said, kissing him on top of his curly head. Then she told him she would be waiting for him on the park bench under the silver maple, and watched him pedal away, the scarf flowing behind him. For a moment, she thought of calling him back and taking the scarf away, or at least retying it, for fear of it getting caught in the spokes. But she didn't, and this reflection would later haunt her.

There was only one witness. A young girl screamed, but when Marina looked up and saw that it was not Oliver, she quickly went back to working on her layout. The girl ran to her mother, crying in Spanish, and Marina noticed that the woman looked alarmed as she cried out to her friends, mothers and nannies all around. Someone yelled "911." It was only then that Marina realized that she couldn't see Oliver anywhere.

Joining the throng of adults and children running in the general direction of the bushes that bordered the bicycle path, she pushed her way through a small crowd that had gathered. In the center of the crowd lay her son, inert and disoriented. He was tangled in the brush, his hair matted with dirt, his clothes torn, and blood on his face. Nearby, the rear wheel of his up-ended bicycle spun listlessly. Marina dropped down and took him in her arms.

"Who did this to you?" she cried. "Oh God." She looked around at the crowd of curious spectators. "Who did this to him?" she screamed.

After some prompting from her mother, the little girl explained that she saw older boys hurting him. They ran away after the girl had screamed. It was ascertained that they were around twelve years old. A couple of the fathers went off in search of the boys while the police were called. Marina held Oliver in her arms and tried to comfort him.

"Shhh," she whispered to him, "shhhh." It was mostly from habit, since it was actually she who couldn't stop weeping.

Hours later, in the dim twilight of her bedroom, Marina watched over Oliver as he lay sleeping in her bed under a mound of blankets. His breathing was calm and steady. He had been given a mild sedative, a "sleep aid" as it was called by the courteous ER doctor who had examined him. Now, after being bathed and dressed, he lay peacefully asleep, and it almost seemed like any other night. The only evidence of the brutality inflicted upon her son was a half-moon slash across his right cheek that the doctor told her, as reassuringly as possible, he was doubtful would scar. Doubtful, not certain. With all of her desperation, she willed it to disappear, knowing how the scar would serve as a constant tormenting reminder that she hadn't been there to stave off his attackers.

Until today, she had been unwavering in her belief that she

was doing the right thing by her son, by letting him be who he was—even as it brought him closer to the other gender, transforming him daily, step by step, from a son into a daughter. But now, staring at the half-moon mark on his cheek, she looked ahead to the continuum of what life held for her child with dread. If a six-year-old could inspire such savagery, what would he endure at sixteen? At twenty-six? It seemed to her then that the world was a place of dark and wet menace, like some underground cave, and as a parent she had done nothing more than thrust her child into its mouth, lanternless, and wish him the best. "There is such a thing as being *too* liberal," she had once overheard a mother sneer to her friend as she and Oliver strode past them on a school tour. Oliver had insisted on wearing his "Cinderella" slippers and crown that day, and he held on to her hand oblivious and confident even as he had teetered on the plastic heels. Before, Marina had taken these people on, challenged them to say more. But now the troubling thought occurred to her: What if they were right?

As she walked out of her bedroom, her eye caught the floral scarf hanging on the back of the door, the same one that Oliver had wrapped around his waist that afternoon. She held it in her hands for a moment, feeling the fear and anger rise up inside of her, and then she stormed into the kitchen and grabbed a giant black trash bag from under the sink. She stuffed the scarf in the bag. Then, with bag in hand, she walked upstairs to Oliver's room. Every dress, tunic, and skirt went into the bag. Sweeping through the room with grim precision, she threw away the tiny pots of lip gloss and nail polish that had been lifted from her drawers. Next came the plush unicorns, stuffed ponies, and kittens. Anything pink, purple, sparkling, glittering, or heart-shaped was taken. The last items she put in the bag were the princess dresses, the matching jeweled plastic heels, and his wand. When she was done, she sat on the floor of the barren room, breathless, feeling as her mother must have felt when her little brother's room was stripped clean after a life-threatening asthma attack. "It's for his own good," her mother had said when Marina's little brother cried for the stuffed goose he had cuddled since birth. "Safety first."

Most nondeciduous plants can survive without light for a few days. But after a week of halted photosynthesis, the chlorophyll dwindles to a disastrous level, the plant's leaves brown and fall off, and soon the plant withers and dies.

Upon finding his world stripped of every trace of femininity, Oliver initially responded with incredulity and outrage. He railed against his once true ally with a frightening furor, only to be met again and again by Marina's steely resolve. He cried, cajoled, and negotiated. He threatened with sustained bouts of holding his breath until he swooned. And then, like the maple leaves that burn the brightest before they lose their color and fall to the earth, so did Oliver languish.

It was following a particularly ragged battle over a shell-pink angora sweater with an embellished rhinestone collar that Oliver had obviously stolen from a classmate and then hidden behind his headboard that Marina lost it. Overwhelmed by frustration when Oliver refused to return the sweater and apologize, she used the last vestige of power she felt she wielded over him. She threatened to cut his hair.

Oliver stared at her, disbelief mingling with fear.

"Please don't, Mommy," he pleaded. "I'll give it back. I'll say I'm sorry. And I won't fight anymore. I promise."

He was true to his word. He stopped fighting—but he also stopped *being*. He became complacent and absent. Marina felt as if her child had been taken from her, replaced by this mild, compliant ghost. And though Marina was a woman who had spent the greater part of her life resolutely single, for the first time she felt the ache of being truly alone.

"It's your turn!" Charlotte called out after swinging herself across the rings. She had finally grasped the concept of momentum and how it carried her from ring to ring like a bird in flight, and her face glowed with the rush of triumph. Oliver sat a few feet away, pointedly ignoring her as he traced random shapes in the sand with a stick. He wore khaki shorts and a solid gray T-shirt like a wrongly convicted prisoner facing a life of incarceration. Regardless of the fact that Marina had purchased an entire new wardrobe for him full of interesting graphic shirts in vibrant colors, Oliver deliberately sought out the same shorts and gray T-shirt every day, even taking them out of the laundry hamper before they had gone through the wash, as if to announce his resignation and reproach to Marina.

"Come on, Ollie!" Charlotte stood in front of him with her bare feet planted in the sand.

Marina knelt down and rubbed her son's back through his gray T-shirt. He swatted her hand away and went back to his shapes.

"I think you should maybe just go again, sweetie," Marina told the girl who was now impatiently hopping on one foot in front of Oliver. "He's going to sit this one out." Charlotte glanced from Marina to her father, who stood a slight distance away.

"Go on, Charlotte," Phillip said. "Oliver is taking a break."

Marina had been avoiding Phillip for weeks, but she had been caught by a phone number that she didn't recognize and mistakenly thought was her pharmacy. In her hurry to get off the phone, she agreed to a playdate with Charlotte but insisted that they meet at another park, without explanation. It was clear that Phillip intuited her reluctance to engage; Marina just let him assume that it was due to the kiss, which now seemed to her embarrassingly inconsequential.

Phillip walked over to Marina and sat down in the sand next to her.

"Hey," he said. "Why don't we let them play together and we can go catch up?"

"They *are* playing together," she replied without looking at him. "If you want to sit down somewhere and make phone calls, go ahead. I can watch the two of them."

Phillip leaned back in an unconscious protective move. "No, I'm fine. I don't have . . . I just meant . . ."

"I'm staying here," she said.

"Daddy!" Charlotte hopped up, trying unsuccessfully to reach the rings on her own. "Help me up!" Phillip stood and lingered for a moment beside Marina, who was hunched over Oliver like a shell.

"Daddy!" Charlotte whined.

He shook his head slightly and walked over to give his daughter a boost. She swung across the rings again, grinning; when she reached the end, he held up his arms and she fell into them.

"Oliver doesn't want to play with me anymore," Charlotte said, ostensibly as a secret but loud enough for her friend to hear.

Phillip glanced over at Oliver, who kept his head down. If he heard, he gave no indication.

It was Marina who spoke up. "That's not true, is it, Ollie? You want to play with your friend, don't you?" Oliver shrugged. He reached out his hand, erasing the shapes he made in the sand, and then began drawing them again.

"Ollie," Marina urged, "if you don't play with Charlotte, she's going to think that you don't want to be friends."

Oliver shrugged again, remaining silent.

In the weeks since his surrender, it felt to Marina as though she were watching him die. In a way, she was. She had effectively killed Olivia by excising her from their lives, though the husk of the living, breathing body of Oliver remained. She was reminded of attending her great-grandmother's open-casket funeral as a child. Marina had stared in bewilderment, transfixed by the immobile body of the woman who had been teaching her how to crochet just days before. She waited for her great-grandmother to move and break the spell, until at last her parents nudged her along, embarrassed by her behavior.

"I was waiting for Nana to move," she had explained in a voice a little too loud.

"Don't be silly," her mother had whispered. "Nana isn't there. It's only her body. Nana's gone to heaven."

Now Marina stared at her son with the same equivocal hope, willing him to return to her, fearing that in her resolve to save his life, she had effectively extinguished it. Where had her son gone to, she wondered, and how could she call him back?

On a Saturday morning in August, she left Oliver at home with the neighbor girl, a sweet-natured teenager whom Marina had known since she was a girl, and took the opportunity to run errands. She was waiting at the coffeehouse counter after having placed her order when her eye happened upon a dress in the shop window next door. It was a children's clothing store named Bees and Buttercups. A broad gilded sign hung above the entrance featuring a plump bumblebee grasping a flower in his anthropomorphic hand. With the school year beginning, all of the clothes on display were imbued with the hopefulness of the new and unknown. The dress was light cotton, with petal sleeves, a pin-tucked bodice, and a silk ribbon tied at the waist. A pair of red leather Mary-Janes were set on the vintage suitcase display next to the dress, delicately crossed at the toes as though in an expression of girlish flirtation.

Marina stepped back into the coffeehouse and took a section

of a newspaper that had been left on a table by the door. As she maneuvered her way through the crowd of people, she happened to see Phillip hunched over a too-small table with a woman who, even from the back, Marina could tell was his wife.

Before she could find a suitable hiding place, Phillip's eyes met hers. He blinked and raised his arm in a half wave. His wife spun around and looked to see where he was waving.

Marina took a deep breath and stopped by the table. She deliberately looked at his wife first.

"Hi. How are you?"

Phillip's wife ran her hand through her hair, and Marina could tell that she couldn't recall her name. She waited a second to see if Phillip would introduce her. He didn't.

"I'm Marina. Oliver's mom. Charlotte's friend?"

Phillip's wife smiled and nodded. "Yes. Charlotte talks about Oliver all the time," she said. "I'm Greta. I know we've met, but . . . nice to meet you again."

Marina glanced over at Phillip who stared down dully at his empty coffee cup.

"Large Americano for Marina!" the young man behind the counter called out. "Marina!"

"That's me," Marina said, turning to leave. "Have a good weekend, you two."

Phillip looked up at her then. "Thank you," he said.

She walked out with her coffee in hand and straight into the shop next door. Up and down the aisles she strode, trying to find something that might please Oliver. She held up a little T-shirt with the Ramones on it, hoodies with PRAY FOR SURF hand-embroidered on the sleeves, small porkpie hats for parents who, she supposed, wanted to fashion their male offspring to look like the Rat Pack in miniature.

A mother stood at the back of the store outside the fitting room while the elderly saleswoman folded a brightly hued sweater. They chatted about when the new collection was expected and if it was worth waiting for everything to go on sale. After a moment, the mother poked her head behind the plum velvet curtain.

"Do you need any help in there, honey?"

"No. I can do it myself!" came the insistent reply from behind the curtain.

The mother laughed and retreated. She picked up a catalogue and thumbed through it. "She's always been so independent," she said. "From the time she could speak, I swear to God!"

The curtain parted and out stepped the little girl. She shyly tucked her dark hair behind one ear and modeled the white eyelet dress, turning this way and that while the women sighed and ahhed as though they were seeing the girl in her wedding dress for the first time.

The mother clapped her hands together. "That will be just *perfect* at Mom-Mom's party, won't it?"

The girl beamed. "I love it, Mommy. I *love* it!"

While her mother handed over her credit card, the girl happily examined the charm bracelets and other trinkets, holding them up to the light and then putting them back.

"I didn't think we would find the perfect one so fast!" the

mother told the saleswoman. "I just hope she doesn't grow out of it before the party!"

Marina approached the saleswoman as the pair exited the store hand in hand.

"May I help you?" the saleswoman asked Marina.

"Yes," Marina said. "I'd like to buy the dress in the window."

"Of course," the saleswoman said. She walked to the display and stepped up on the platform to retrieve the dress.

While the saleswoman removed the dress from the mannequin, Marina glanced around the shop, marveling at the striking combinations of color, cut, and cloth. Look at all this prettiness, Marina thought. Look at all this light.

"I knew this wouldn't last up there long," the saleswoman said as she smoothed out the fabric of the dress. "It's just darling. Would you like it gift wrapped?"

She brought the dress to Marina, who touched the soft silk of the ribbon between her thumb and finger.

"Yes, please," Marina said. "It's for my daughter."

URSA MINOR

FOR THE GREATER PART of his twenties and half of his thirties, Peter Layton's longest-standing relationship was with a young male polar bear named Pooka. Pooka was not a real polar bear but an animated one, and though Peter's life was inextricably linked with Pooka's, Peter and Pooka never actually met. Theirs was an intimate relationship consummated in postproduction by a team of highly skilled computer animators. Peter worked with a script in front of a "green screen" while a director and skeleton crew guided Peter from gaffer-taped mark to mark on the concrete sound stage in Queens, New York. But to all the children of the world the places that Peter and Pooka visited were legion.

Of course, when Peter first arrived in New York City upon graduating from Yale Drama, the last thing he had on his mind was children's television. His turn as Trigorin in *The Seagull* had been hailed as "superlative" (according to the college newspaper), matched only by his interpretation of Richard

Roma in *Glengarry Glen Ross*, in which local reviewers found in Peter that intangible fusion of intensity and irresistible insouciance—in short, the elusive charisma that is the golden ticket for any young actor. He moved into a Williamsburg loft with a couple of his former classmates and gave himself a year to concentrate on his indisputably promising acting career before even considering a day job.

At first, everything seemed to go as planned. He landed a respectable off-off Broadway job within a month of living in New York. It was an original play written by a young playwright (and former Yalie), produced by a theater company comprised of moonlighting Hollywood actors with serious theater pretensions. The play was middling at best, but Peter was extremely well received and clearly shone above the other considerably more experienced thespians. Though the play was not financially lucrative, it managed to secure him representation with a small boutique agency specializing in theater, and *New York* magazine chose his picture to front a featured article showcasing young talent.

And then nothing.

He got plenty of auditions and a respectable amount of callbacks, but the feedback was always frustratingly difficult to decipher. "Too intense." "Uncommitted." "Distracted." "Too good-looking." "Not good-looking enough." Among the most maddening was when a ginger-haired, pockmarked casting director, pressed by Peter's agent as to why he hadn't called his client back for a bit part in an independent movie, confided, "He just didn't *sparkle*."

The agent passed this on to Peter as an accusation.

"What am I? Fucking Christmas-tree tinsel?" Peter vented to his roommate Ben as they walked to the L train. Ben worked at a juice bar in the East Village and commuted daily.

Ben shrugged. "I'm a Jew. We don't know from tinsel."

"I was good. I know I was. The way the writer looked at me when I was shaking their hands—"

"You shake their hands?" Ben asked.

"Yeah," Peter said. "Of course I do. Don't you?"

Ben shook his head. "No."

"Wait! What, you just leave?" Peter wasn't through venting, but he was intrigued. "You just wave or something?"

"I don't want them to think I'm kissing their ass," Ben said. "Even though I would gladly kiss their ass if it would get me in someone's movie. I'd put my tongue right in there—"

"All right, all right." Peter laughed. "I don't think that's Kosher."

"I would kiss the ass of a pig on the Sabbath if it would get me hired," Ben went on. Commiserating about auditions and rejections was one of the best things about being friends with someone who struggled with the same ridiculous career. Peter was alternately amused and relieved whenever Ben would rant about losing out on a part. And while it shamed Peter to admit it, he was occasionally consoled by the fact that Ben had experienced even less success upon leaving Yale than Peter had. Over the years, Ben had booked fewer than a handful of parts in tiny productions, and the week before, Peter had come across an application for the LSAT on the kitchen counter while picking up his mail. Before too long, Peter figured, his friend and confidant would formally abandon his stalled acting career and head back to school to learn the family profession.

When they arrived at the dingy staircase that led down into the subway station, Peter stopped and began rummaging through his backpack.

"You go on," he told Ben. "I got a meeting here."

"No shit?" Ben turned around. "And here I was feeling sorry for you."

Peter retrieved a Chinese-food menu with an address scrawled across it. "You can still feel sorry for me. It's for a children's television show."

Ben laughed. "You're about as kid-friendly as an unsupervised wading pool."

"Thanks for the vote of confidence" Peter said, and headed west. He turned and yelled, "Yo! Bring home some wheatgrass!"

Ben waved his hand over his shoulder as he descended underground.

That night, Peter's agent left a message on his answering machine. He was being called back.

A week later, he was hired.

The flight to Los Angeles was packed and seemed more full of babies and children than usual. Peter wore his sunglasses and Yankees cap and made sure to speak as little as possible so as to attract the least amount of attention. It was over two years since he had left *Peter & Pooka* in disgrace, though according to the press release, Peter had left after fifteen years to "pursue other ventures." The network vehemently denied that there were drugs involved so as not to sully the magnificently successful brand that was *Peter & Pooka*, and except for the *New York Post* staff photographer who had snapped Peter leaving Beth Israel Hospital—where he had been treated for "exhaustion"—and printed it with the crushingly emasculating headline IS PETER POOPED? his reputation as the squeaky-clean companion of Pooka remained intact.

The scandal surrounding Peter's departure was quickly and willfully forgotten by the program's loyal following, a forgiving group of fans primarily under the age of five. Their mothers forgave Peter, too, and perhaps were even titillated by his transgression. For years these same mothers watched Peter frolic in foreign countries, nibbling food they would never try, learning about exotic cultures they would never visit, and they were charmed by the seeming guilelessness and enthusiasm that Peter projected. Just when their lives had begun to be weighed down by the exhausting pressures of motherhood, and as their husbands retreated into earning for a family that they would rarely see, Peter offered them a fantasy. He was as much of a companion to the mothers as to their preschool-aged children. He embodied a collective emotional fantasy—a lovable man-child who, unlike their husbands, never got angry, never withdrew or neglected them. He was always there to distract and charm, clearly intelligent and reassuringly familiar. But he wasn't real. Until that picture surfaced in the *Post*, Peter was indistinguishable from his funny, sunny counterpart, and then overnight he became a real man who had become intimately reacquainted with his shadow. The network fired him, but the mothers secretly loved him for it.

Squeezing past the legs of a businessman on the aisle and an acne-afflicted teenager with headphones in the center seat, Peter sat by the window and stared out at the rain-soaked tarmac. It had been raining for days in New York, and he felt a twinge of hope as he visualized the mild weather in California. He was planning to stay with his twin sister, Lindsay, who had moved to Los Angeles years ago and had since found considerable success as a landscape artist for the affluent beach set. Lindsay had little formal training, but she had the gift of an intuitive eye inherited from their mother—a seemingly effortless way of creating an atmosphere of style and ease. Lindsay showed her clients a lifestyle as much as where to plant the perennials.

She had been dogging her brother for weeks to visit, knowing how difficult life had become for him in New York. And although Peter had no want of money after fifteen years on the television show and could easily have paid for a hotel, his sister insisted that he stay with her. So he took her up on her offer, comforted by the thought of spending time with the one person to whom he felt he never had to explain anything.

"Excuse me? Sir? Mr. Layton?"

Peter turned to see a flight attendant kneeling in the aisle next to the businessman. She was a trim woman with bright-pink lipstick and streaked blond hair pulled back in a severe twist.

"Would you mind coming with me?" When she smiled, Peter noticed a smear of pink lipstick smudged against her white teeth.

Peter was startled. "Is there something wrong?"

His two flying companions looked at him with vague interest. The teenager took the headphones out of his ears and squinted at him.

"Dude, I know you," he said.

The flight attendant stood up and smoothed out her skirt. "I can carry your bag if it's in the overhead."

"No," Peter said. "I have my bag here." He grabbed the magazines that he had stashed in the seat pocket and squeezed his way back out, apologizing as he tripped over the businessman's legs.

"You're that polar-bear guy!" the teenager said. A few heads turned in his direction. "Trippy," he heard the boy say as he hurried down the aisle after the flight attendant.

There was a group of four other flight attendants waiting for him in the galley closest to the front, and they squealed when Peter entered, concerned and confused.

"I'm Marcie," the first attendant said. "We have an extra seat for you in first class, but we didn't want to say anything in front of the other passengers."

"Oh," Peter said. "That's nice." He smiled at the grinning women.

One of the flight attendants, who stood at least two inches taller than him in flat shoes, grasped his hand. "But it's on condition that you sign this for my son." She giggled and thrust out a ticket printout and a green Sharpie, wrapping Peter's fingers around it. "He loves you. *Loves* you. He sleeps with Pooka and dressed like you for Halloween two years in a row. I'm not kidding!"

Peter obediently began to sign his name on the ticket. Another of the women, short and stout with a frizzy mop of hair dyed a burgundy color that never would have occurred in nature, took a steady stream of pictures with her cell phone.

"He looked so cute in his striped purple turtleneck," the flight-attendant mother for whom Peter was signing the ticket told her coworkers.

Peter handed the ticket back and looked to the other women. A brunette with eyes that seemed far too large for her face handed him a ticket of her own.

"Can you make it out to Sailor? She's my niece."

"Sailor? That's an interesting name," Peter said. He was overtired from not having slept the night before and for a moment could not remember how to spell "Sailor."

"I know, it had to grow on me," the woman confessed. "Her daddy is a Marine."

"*I* didn't know that," Marcie said. "That's just precious!"

An Asian man poked his head in the galley and asked for a glass of water by motioning with his hands, pantomiming taking a drink. The burgundy-haired flight attendant who clearly had seniority shooed him away with her hands. "You need to take your seat now."

The man pointed to his seat, where his wife sat with a baby in her lap. He made the motion again for water.

"Sir, you really need to take your seat. *Now,*" the woman said. She put her hand on his back and another on his shoulder and pushed him in the direction of his seat. "Go. Move. Sit."

The man walked back to his seat and sat down.

"Sorry about that," she said to Peter, laughing. "Some people just can't follow rules."

Peter looked at the man, who was being questioned by his wife in Korean. As the husband unleashed his frustration on his wife, their baby began to wail. The passengers nearby rolled their eyes and covered their ears.

"I think the water was for the baby," Peter said.

"They always say that," the woman told him.

The captain came on the loudspeaker, announcing in a friendly Texan drawl the plane's position in line for takeoff. Peter felt a surge of relief knowing that soon he would be released from the women's clutches. He posed for a picture with each flight attendant individually, then for a group picture snapped on self-timer with a point-and-shoot camera precariously perched on top of the galley cart. At their urging he acted out the show's stock phrase—"Pep up, Pooka! Peter's here!"—and then was shown by Marcie to first class, collapsing into his seat, hot and flushed, his hair sticking in ribbons to the perspiration on his forehead.

He felt as though he had never before paid so much for a ticket in his life.

Upon exiting the terminal at baggage claim, Peter was smacked in the face with a gust of hot, tobacco-scented air. All of the

smokers stood huddled in groups, sucking on the cigarettes as
if they were oxygen. Peter, a casual smoker back when he was
at Yale and later when he was a promising actor in New York—
and then secretly for the past fifteen years because of clause
number 34b in his contract that stated that he would be fined
in increasing increments if a picture of him smoking was ever
published—walked over to what looked to be a sixtysomething
career smoker and asked to bum a cigarette. When the end was
ignited and Peter got a good pull, he thanked her and walked
to the curb, watching the police officers in bright-green safety
vests harass the drivers and arbitrarily ticket them if they failed
to move along with sufficient haste. Peter counted at least three
teary reunions interrupted by one of these stocky, ill-tempered
oafs. One longhaired young man in a surfing hoodie, who had
clearly been looking forward to his reunion with his girlfriend,
cocked his head and wrinkled his brow.

"What the fuck is your problem?" he said.

The cop reddened in the face and advanced toward him.
"You want a ticket?"

"No, I don't want a ticket." The man stepped in front of his
dreadlocked girlfriend. "I want to know why you have to be
such an asshole."

His girlfriend, so thin that the bones of her clavicles stuck out
like butter knives, tugged at his collar and tried to get him to
lift her suitcase.

The cop pulled out his pad and began writing the ticket just
as Peter heard Lindsay beep her horn.

His sister sat in the worn leather driver's seat in a white vintage Mercedes convertible with the top down. "Hey, Pumpkin-eater!" She smiled at her brother. He tossed the cigarette in the gutter, threw his small bag in the backseat, and hopped in the front.

She was wearing an off-white bohemian sundress with the collar embroidered in black. It looked like something that he'd seen on a Greek island or on Ibiza, where he had spent one marijuana-infused summer flush with his first-year earnings from the show. Her arms were tan, and her long, dark curly hair had fewer silver streaks running though them than his had.

He leaned in to kiss her on the cheek.

"Welcome to L.A., honey," she said. "I'm glad you're here."

"Thanks," he said. "Glad to be here. Glad to be anywhere but New York right now."

She glanced in her rearview mirror and merged into the traffic. "You smell like an ashtray," she said.

Peter rummaged around in her glove box for a mint or gum.

"Do you have one?" she said. "I've been dying for a smoky treat all day."

"Oh. I thought you quit."

"I did," she said. "That's why I don't have any, silly!"

Peter closed the glove box and leaned back. "Sorry, I bummed one from a lady out front."

"*Tant pis,*" Lindsay said. "Hey, did I tell you? Didier is really looking forward to seeing you.

Peter nodded, uncommitted. Didier was Lindsay's boyfriend going on ten years now. The Frenchman did not wish to marry his sister, claiming that marriage was "*beaucoup trop bourgeois.*" He also chose not to have a green card, so that he never legally had the right to work in the country. Instead, he took pictures for obscure publications in France for little to no money and lived off Peter's sister, alternately adoring and despising her, depending on the fluctuations of his ego. Infuriatingly, his sister remained inexplicably devoted to him. Peter suspected that Didier had become an accessory of sorts in her fashion-driven lifestyle. He looked good in the slim bespoke suits that he had tailored for himself when he was required to leave the country every three months, stopping in either London or France for a week before returning to the U.S. on another three-month tourist visa. His ties came from Charvet in Paris, his suits from Henry Poole, a Saville Row tailor with a self-professed connection to royalty, and his monogramed, made-to-order shirts from Brooks Brothers. Peter had to admit that for all of his sister's money that Didier invested in his wardrobe, he somehow managed to never look as though he was trying.

"So he's in town this week?" Peter asked as they accelerated onto the freeway ramp.

"Just got back from Paris last week. He picked up these amazing Charlotte Perriand sconces from this lady downstairs from his mother. Crazy. She had no idea what they were."

Peter nodded. He had no idea what they were either—neither the designer nor the word "sconce"—but he figured that in Lindsay's world of style and design, this was a big deal.

Peter grinned as the hot Los Angeles air flooded the car. Feeling warm for the first time in months, he stretched out and closed his eyes.

"Tired?" Lindsay asked.

"Mmm," Peter murmured.

"Hey, I wanted to ask if you mind, but I'm having a few people over for dinner tonight. Not a huge deal."

Peter opened his eyes. He felt the startling surge of discomfort he often felt when confronted by the prospect of being around successful people. Lindsay weaved her car in and out of traffic, cutting off at least three cars. A hybrid Honda honked its horn at her and its driver flipped her off.

"Sorry!" She waved her ringed hand at the driver and blew him a kiss.

"What kind of people?" Peter asked her.

"What kind of people where?" she said.

Lindsay was conspicuously forgetful. Peter had been alternately amused and annoyed by this since they were kids.

"The party that you were talking about less than thirty seconds ago?"

"Oh you know, a mixture. A potpourri," she said. "All good."

Peter didn't feel particularly buoyed by her description, but he also knew that Lindsay's parties were a part of her work and didn't feel that he had the right to refuse. He was a guest in their home—at least until he moved to a hotel, which now seemed inevitable.

"I might duck out, go see a movie or something, if that's all right with you."

Lindsay frowned at him and almost missed braking as the Subaru in front of her abruptly slowed down.

"Don't do that, P. I'm having this party for you!"

"For me? Oh God. Why didn't you ask me? Or give me a day to—"

"To what, to decide you hate it here and run back to New York? I want to introduce you to people. People you should know."

By the time they had pulled off the freeway onto the Pacific Coast Highway and Peter had breathed in the ocean air, managing to catch a glimpse of the great ball of sun as it sank behind the water, he had forgiven his sister for attempting to reinvent him. It was her business, after all, to help make people look better than they were, so why not him?

Lindsay's house had changed significantly since the last time Peter had seen it. He had given her the money for the down payment a decade ago, after *Peter & Pooka* had just become a phenomenon. Lindsay was just beginning her career and chose a tear-down in Venice, California, at the perfect time—predating the enormous gentrification of the area, perhaps even helping to initiate it. Rather than destroy the house entirely, Lindsay had modified it so that, though practically unrecognizable, it kept certain key elements: wavy old windows, exposed beams salvaged from an old Venice pier. She even left an enormous old fig tree that grew in what was originally the front yard of the house, building the additions around it. The concrete floor had drains in it so that when it rained, the water channeled through the floor and into a complicated watering system that cycled into the garden.

Peter lay down on the bed in the guesthouse and closed his eyes. People would be arriving in a couple of hours for the party, but his eyes burned with the pull of sleep. He knew that if he fell asleep now, there was little chance he would be able to rally for tonight, so he forced himself out of bed and dropped to the floor, halfheartedly attempting push-ups.

He was fifteen into his set when the unmistakable odor of a cigar wafted through the open window. Peter parted the shade and there was Didier reclining in a chair under an umbrella reading *Le Monde*, puffing on a cigar. The thought of having a conversation with Didier was unappealing, so he backed away from the window to finish his push-ups and shower, hoping Didier would be gone by the time he was finished.

Under the showerhead, he let the water beat down on his head and shoulders. The pressure was good and went a long way to wash away the flight experience that he imagined as a film covering his body. He was about to get out of the shower when the thought occurred to him to masturbate; briefly he debated whether it would wake him up for the party or lull him further into somnolence. By then his hand had absently begun the task so he attempted to conjure up an image that would get it done. His ex-girlfriend, Sue Ming, flickered in his mind. She was a child-development researcher hired by the network to make sure that the show followed certain guidelines, and she spent a lot of time on the set peering at notes on a yellow legal pad through blue vintage cat-eye glasses. For years he had been wildly attracted to her, but as soon as they slept with each other for the first time, her allure all but evaporated for Peter, and he found himself having to think of other women and situations in order to perform. It was strange now to have Sue and her glasses come to mind almost two years after they had said good-bye. He tried to picture her in the gray tank top and little lacy boy-shorts that she used to wear to bed, but almost simultaneously, he remembered her face after she let herself into his apartment, when she found him asleep next to a woman he had met the night before at a bar in Greenpoint. What was her name? Karen? Kelly? It was a "K" name for sure, but everything else was hazy. He woke up and Sue was standing in the doorway with coffee and croissants from the café down the street, while the mascara-smeared K girl slept naked next to him, drooling on the pillow.

"I don't understand," is all Sue said. "I don't understand." And she really did look confused.

He was confused as well, not really sure how he and the girl had ended up at his place after he had given Sue his key only the week before. He vaguely remembered something about roommates and a college dorm, and after all the tequila shots he had ordered for everyone at the bar, borough hopping had seemed unappealing. So they stumbled to his apartment in Park Slope, drank more tequila, and he remembered little else.

There was no scene. Sue simply set the bag with the croissants on the bureau along with the coffee and walked out. She mailed his key back to him the following week.

The thought of Sue Ming, her glasses and her pained, incomprehensive expression did little to advance the situation at hand, so he switched to the memory of a porn film that he had seen when he was thirteen years old. The woman had frizzy hair, enormous natural breasts—or so he assumed, since it pre-dated the proliferation of everything fake—and her face wore a permanently lascivious expression. He saw her open her legs and stare up at the man who, if memory served, was wearing a doctor's coat and horn-rimmed glasses, and said in a voice that sounded incongruously sweet in comparison to the sexy sneer, "Don't you want it?"

Peter closed his eyes and concentrated. He switched places with the doctor and walked toward her. "Yes, I want it," he said. Putting his hands on her knees he pushed them wider, and then in the shower the water ran scalding hot. "Fuck!" he yelled and jumped to the side. He waited for a moment and then tentatively ran his hand under the shower to see if it had cooled. Stepping back under the shower, he tried to envision the scene once again. "Don't you want it?" the woman said. But this time something was different. Her hair was in a twist instead of loose. He readjusted to the change and coaxed himself back up. "Yes," he said as Dr. Peter. He unzipped his pants and watched her eyes grow large in a gratuitous expression of appreciation—and then the water ran cold. He stepped to the side, trying desperately to keep the fantasy in play. Back under the showerhead, he resumed, stepping toward her as she lay back in anticipation, but just as he finally entered her with a moan, the water ran blistering hot again.

"Fuck, fuck, FUCK!" he screamed. He jumped to the side, and his left foot landed on a bar of soap that had softened. As he fell, his legs landed in some version of a split, and in a panic his arms flailed upward, managing to knock over all of the bottles of shower gel, shampoos, and conditioners lined up on the ledge. One of the bottles shattered and a shard of glass embedded itself in his big toe. He turned off the shower, grabbed a towel, and wrapped it around himself. Hopping across the room on one foot, he sat down on the bed and attempted to remove the shard without tweezers.

"*Ça va?*" He heard Didier's voice calling from outside. "Everything okay?"

He managed to remove the glass, cutting his fingers in the process, and then opened the door for Didier, who looked up from his paper with bland interest.

"I heard you crying," he said.

Didier often mixed up his verbs in English, usually just choosing the one that sounded closest to the French.

"Your shower's got a problem," Peter said. "I just about killed myself in there."

Didier nodded. "*Oui.* I've been telling your sister that she needs to have a *plombier* come, but she forgets." He puffed on his cigar and exhaled slowly, admiring the smoke as it dissipated in the air.

The guests began to arrive at dusk, one by one at first and then all at once. Peter stood alone under an outdoor heater. He noticed how much color everyone had and how healthy and smiling they seemed. He felt very wan and pale in comparison and wished that his sister had waited at least a day to throw the party. But Lindsay had always been overly enthusiastic and impatient. He remembered the year that she talked him into opening all of the Christmas presents in advance that their mother had stashed in the back of their parents' closet. "Come on, you know you want to," she baited him. "What difference does it make if we know now, really?" They were eleven years old, and even now he was impressed by the simplicity of her argument. Not, "Why don't we check, and that way you'll know if they got you the Atari?" followed up by "How are you going to know what to hint for?" Lindsay's argument was brutal in its simplicity: *What difference does it make?* It seemed irrefutable at the time. He was dumbfounded at having experienced his first existential crisis. By stating that it made no difference if they opened the gifts then or on Christmas Day, or any other day, it stood to reason that nothing mattered. If Christmas was like any other day, then what about Halloween? The Fourth of July? What about the day he was born? He looked at his sister's face, flushed and bright at the prospect of the espionage, and agreed to do it. So they opened every present, and then immediately and painstakingly wrapped them all back up afterward, feeling solemn and depressed. Lindsay had looked on the edge of tears that she had ruined their Christmas, but Peter told her it was okay. He vowed then, the first of many times, never to be controlled by her impatience. And yet here he was again.

Lindsay smiled, graciously accepting bouquets of flowers and bottles of wine from her guests. She passed the wine on to Didier, who had been born to the parents of a fading haute bourgeois, a generation that while squandering the money of its forebears was nevertheless schooled in the best of everything no longer affordable. He took the wine and set about uncorking each bottle with an almost religious reverence. Peter watched as he opened, sniffed, and then displayed the bottles with precision along the center of the low outdoor dining table.

Lindsay came over and grabbed Peter by the shoulder, eagerly nudging him toward a bald man wearing shaded glasses. "Quintin, this is my brother, Peter," Lindsay said.

The bald man flashed a smile. "How do you do?" he said as his eyes flitted from Peter's eyes, down his body, and then back to his eyes in less than a second. "Now, where has she been hiding you?"

"He's my big brother!" Lindsay said, touching the man lightly on the cheek. "Born a whole three and a half minutes before me!"

"Nice to meet you," Peter said.

A severe-looking woman with a Louise Brooks bob, deep-hooded eyes, and a slash of a red mouth came over. Quintin put his arm around the woman while still looking at Peter.

"This is my wife, Rita," he said.

"Rita is a phenomenal artist," Lindsay said. "Those sketches you were admiring in the hallway? Hers."

"You are too kind," Rita lowered her lids and smiled. Her pointy canines jutted out, giving her the look of something feral.

Peter had no idea what sketches Lindsay was referring to, but he nodded and smiled anyway.

"And Quintin works at Warners," Lindsay said. "You *must* cast my brother!"

"You're an actor?" It was a question that sounded declarative, and Peter felt that he could already sense the man's interest wane.

"He's incredible." Lindsay linked her arm in Peter's and leaned her head affectionately on his shoulder. "I'm trying to get him to move out here."

"From where?" Quintin asked. Peter watched the man's eyes dart around as he surveyed who else was at the party.

"New York," Lindsay said.

"Oh, where in New York?" Rita asked. "We still keep a place in SoHo."

"Brooklyn," Peter said. "Would you excuse me? I was just going to get a drink. Can I get you anything?"

"No, thank you," Rita said. "I'm going to see what Didier is pouring."

"Have your agent set something up," Quintin said to Peter as he backed away.

"Will do," Peter said. "Thanks."

He walked across the gravel, over the stepping-stones that had been artfully arranged so as to suggest a skyscraper, and into the kitchen to grab a beer. A woman in a fuchsia sari was leaning into the open refrigerator. She turned around and jumped when she saw Peter.

"Oh! Hi there. I was just grabbing some Badoit," she said, holding up the water bottle as if proof.

"You didn't happen to see any beer in there, did you?" Peter asked.

The woman stepped to the side. "Have a look," she said. "You're Lindsay's brother, aren't you?"

"I am," Peter said.

"I'm Vela," the woman said. "Lindsay practices yoga in my studio."

"Oh, yoga. Great," Peter said.

"Do you practice?" Vela set about opening cupboards, looking for a glass.

"No. Can't say I do," Peter said.

"Well, we have a fantastic beginners' class on Tuesday," Vela told him. She located a glass and poured herself some of the French mineral water. "You want some? Oh, right. You were looking for a beer, weren't you?" She laughed, an attractive husky laugh, and put the extra glass back in the cupboard. "Our website is called Chit Yoga."

"Excuse me?" Peter said.

"Philosophically, pure awareness, transcendent consciousness, as in *Sat-chit-ananda*," she explained.

"Oh. *Chit*," Peter said, nodding. "I'll be sure to check you out. I mean *it*. Not you."

Vela laughed again. "You can check me out, too." She winked at him and headed outside. Peter felt the tips of his ears turn red. Vela was garden-variety beautiful, but curiously he was not attracted to her at all. He had always found women with arms more muscular than his intimidating. He located a beer in the refrigerator and went on the hunt for a bottle opener. Lindsay rushed into the kitchen and grabbed him by the shirt.

"No hiding in here!" she scolded.

"Where do you keep your bottle openers?"

She went to a drawer on the opposite side of the kitchen and found one. Grabbing his beer, she opened it for him and threw the cap away. Then she took hold of his arm and pulled him out of the kitchen, back into the throng.

"Isn't Vela great?" Lindsay said. "She said she met you."

"Yeah, she seems nice. Yoga, huh?"

Lindsay leaned in and whispered conspiratorially in his ear. "You should definitely have your agent call Quintin. He just got promoted and if he likes you . . ."

"Okay, Linds. Don't worry about me. Go be a hostess."

He didn't have the heart to tell her that his agent had let him go after the *New York Post* debacle, and he hadn't gotten around to finding another one.

They weaved their way through the crowd of people while Lindsay embraced, kissed, and laughed with her carefully selected mélange of writers, artists, designers, and financiers. She continually tried, and failed, to draw him into the various conversations.

"Sean!" Lindsay threw her arms around a tall man wearing a fitted T-shirt clearly intended to show off his physique. He looked familiar to Peter. "Where's Stella?" Lindsay demanded. "She's coming, isn't she?"

"Parking," the man said. "She won't let me drive her Volt until she gets a dent in it herself."

"Oh, you are too funny," Lindsay said. "Not only does she direct you, but she chauffeurs you around as well. What a lucky boy."

"Lucky and emasculated," Sean said. He smiled at Peter with the look of someone who is used to charming a room with his false modesty. Peter laughed a little too enthusiastically and took the opportunity to retreat before Lindsay had a chance to introduce him. He recognized now that Sean was an actor, primarily known for action movies, but who had recently broken into more serious films with a couple of parts in some carefully chosen independent films. He had married the director of one of them, Stella, a woman fifteen years his senior, and his career had just now reached the watershed moment when an actor has a chance at the best of everything. He was on the list that could get movies made just by agreeing to be in them, regardless of suitability or skill.

Just by looking at him, Peter knew that Sean wasn't a good actor. He would bet money that he had never studied Chekhov, Ibsen, or even Shakespeare, but Peter would also be willing to bet that it would be Sean, this latter-day matinee idol, who would be called by the Public Theater to perform Shakespeare in the Park. He felt the nauseating and all-too-familiar sensations of failure and envy, and he fled the house, looking for a place far enough away from everyone to inhibit conversation but close enough so that he couldn't be accused by his sister of leaving the party.

Outside, the last of the early evening light was evanescing. Someone switched on the outdoor lights, and little bulbs illuminated the garden, giving it the look of a provincial town square in France. Peter wandered through the raised beds of vegetables and herbs. He stopped at a large tomato vine and picked a tomato.

"Isn't it the best scent ever?"

He turned and saw a slender woman with a short blond pixie cut standing next to him.

"The best," Peter said.

"My mother used to grow tomatoes in her garden, and I always thought if I made a perfume, I would make tomato vine one of the notes."

Peter nodded.

"The vines actually smell even better than the tomatoes," she said.

"You make perfume?" Peter asked.

"No, I said *if*."

"Oh, you sounded all professional, with the whole 'notes,' and all."

She laughed. "Maybe that's what I should do. Make perfume," she said. "But don't you have to be famous now to make a perfume?"

"You're not famous?" Peter said. "Forget it, I'm not talking to you. Don't you know there are famous people here at this party!" He turned around and walked a few steps away, then turned back. She was smiling. He noticed her two front teeth overlapping slightly. It was a really nice smile.

"I'm Peter," he said.

"Greta." She gave him her hand and he took it in his. It was small and delicate and for some reason made him think of a little bird.

"Who do you know here?" he asked her.

"No one," she said. "Except Lindsay." She turned and looked at the people milling around the yard, chatting. "You?"

"She's my sister," he said.

"I was wondering," Greta said. "You have the same nose."

Peter self-consciously reached his hand up to touch his nose. He rubbed the bridge of it and then drank the rest of his beer and looked around for somewhere to throw the bottle.

"Here I'll take that," Greta said. She reached out her hand to him and he stared at her, confused.

"What? You'll take my empty beer bottle?"

She withdrew her hand, and he could see the flush of embarrassment on her face.

"Do you often solicit the trash of strangers?" he asked

"It's a habit," she said. "I have a daughter and I always have my hand out. Gum, candy wrappers, food she's chewed up and spit out . . ."

At the mention of her daughter, Peter glanced down at her hand to see if she was wearing a ring. Her hand was bare.

"I have an idea," he said. "Let's go try some of that food over there, and whatever I don't like, I'll just spit in your hand."

Greta threw her head back and laughed, and Peter was surprised at how pleasant it was to hear her laugh.

"You're funny," she said. "I don't think I'm going to stay very long though."

"Don't go," he said.

She looked at him questioningly, and it was his turn to be embarrassed.

"I mean . . . why are you going to go?" he stammered. "Do you have to get home to your kid or something?"

"I don't have to . . ." she said. "She's with her father right now. At *his* place," she added quickly.

"Do me a favor then, and don't go," he said. Standing next to this woman, a stranger, he felt as though he was a man at sea drowning and she a buoy thrown to him as he gulped his last mouthful of saltwater. The intensity of the feeling was so strong that it eclipsed any anxiety or fear of rejection that he should have been feeling. All that mattered to him at that moment was that she not leave him there alone.

She looked slightly rattled, her eyebrows knitting together in consternation. Suddenly, he grew mortified by his outburst and raced through his mind thinking of graceful ways that he could recant. Too many drinks, he could say—though truthfully he'd had only one beer. Jet-lag. Maybe he could pass it off as a joke? He looked down at his shoes as he felt his discomfort creeping through him in the awkward silence. Then he looked up and found her staring back at him with an inscrutable smile on her face.

"I'll stay," she said.

When she did leave the party, less than an hour later and at his prompting, they made their escape together. While Greta said her good-byes and thank-yous to Lindsay, Peter waited for her in the back alley behind the house until she emerged and they ran off down the street with the exultant air of disobedient schoolchildren. They didn't stop running for two full blocks, at which point Greta stopped, laughing and panting. She leaned over, holding her side, pressing the heel of her hand into it.

"I have a stitch," she said. "Ouch!"

Her face was flushed with excitement and pleasure. On impulse, Peter took her face in his hands and kissed her. She kissed him back, timidly at first and then with an intensity that was visceral in its desire. When they broke apart, breathless and shy, no one spoke. Peter took her small hand in his, and together they walked in silence toward the ocean without even knowing for sure in which direction they would find the water.

She was five years older than him, which seemed like little to him but mattered a great deal to Greta. "Oh God. I'm so old," she complained. "I've never been with anyone younger than me."

"Don't you know it's a trend?" he said. "Think of me like a stylish handbag."

It was days later, and having spent nearly every one of them together—at least for a couple of hours—they had fallen into a conversational ease that felt both brand-new yet wholly familiar. For Peter, being with Greta was like being wrapped in a warm towel after emerging cold and shivering from the ocean. They wandered along the Venice boardwalk, past dreadlocked men, tattooed women, skaters, artists, and the homeless. The smells of incense and marijuana and saltwater wafted through the air. As they passed by a "pharmacy," which was nothing more than a rebranded head-shop, a young man in a lab coat passed out flyers in front.

"We're here to help," he said as he pressed one into Greta's hand.

"Thanks," she said. Peter took the flyer from her and dropped it in the first trash can they passed.

"I've never been with someone divorced," he said. "So there's a first for both of us."

"Except I'm not divorced," she said. "Not yet."

Her statement took him off guard. He had assumed that Greta was divorced but realized now that they had carefully avoided the topic. "Well, I've never been with anyone married either," he said lightly, waiting for the laugh. When it didn't come, he looked over and saw the pain in her face. "At least, as far as I know," he added.

"You would know," she said. She quickened her pace slightly and kept her gaze forward. He sped up to stay close to her.

"How recently did you guys separate?" he asked.

"I found out last September that my husband was fucking my daughter's nineteen-year-old violin teacher." She pronounced the word with a staccato sharpness, emphasizing the *k*.

"So, not so recent," he said.

He felt her shiver next to him.

"It feels recent," she said. "It feels like it happened yesterday. Well, maybe not yesterday, but at least last week." She stepped to the side, narrowly missing tripping over the money bowl of a street performer. "We were together for twenty-one years," she said with a sigh. "Married eighteen of them."

Peter nodded as he felt the weight of what she was saying. Twenty-one years. He was fourteen when Greta and her husband were likely doing what he and Greta were doing right now. Falling.

"That's a long time," he said. He winced at the reductiveness of his comment.

"My whole life," she said. She stopped and looked at him. The light from the neon signs flashed across her face. "Hey, you aren't a cheater by any chance, are you? I don't know what we're doing, but before we do . . . just tell me."

"I'm not," he said. She scrutinized his face for a moment and then exhaled. They resumed walking. The abruptness of her question had caught him off guard, and he lied before he could even think of a way to tell her the truth. Though in a way, he felt that there was truth in his statement. Being with Greta inspired in him a desire to be something better than what he was, better than what he had become. Even if this feeling was ephemeral, as love more than often is, he wanted to chase it. Even if it only lasted this week, he told himself, he would hold this vision of his better self in his mind as a reminder of what he could be. Why not start now? He stopped and took a deep breath. Reaching out, he took her by the elbow and pulled her close.

"Greta, I have."

"Have what?"

"Cheated."

He saw her eyes flash and then just as quickly dissolve into a distant and unreachable pain. "Good to know," she said coldly as she set off walking again. He tried to hold her hand, but she shook herself free of his grip, as if he were attempting to hand her a fistful of bees.

"I didn't want to lie to you," he said.

"But you did lie," she said. "That's what it was. A lie." She picked up her pace. He watched her retreating from him and then ran to catch up to her.

"Stop it!" Peter cried out. "Have you never lied? Have you never cheated? On anything? On a math test even? I'm not proud of what I did. But it's not who I am."

She looked at him, and he watched the anger mingling with pain and fear. He stared back at her, refusing to release her gaze. With the superstition of the newly fallen, he felt that if he blinked first, he would lose her. She closed her eyes and shook her head.

"This is silly," she said. "I mean, God. We just met." She half smiled and shrugged her shoulders in a sad sort of resignation.

"And we've already had our first fight," he said. "We don't waste time."

"I'm hungry," she said.

"So am I." He pulled her into him and felt her cheek hot against his chest. He took her shoulders in his hands and held her a short distance away from him to see her face.

He looked at her in wonder. Everything that he owned in the world was three thousand miles away, and yet here was all that he wanted, glorious in its smallness and its brightness, its soft and unwavering trueness. It all came into focus. Colors seemed to burn and fluoresce. Cynics would say that it was chemical—

that this feeling was nothing more than the all-powerful cock-tail of dopamine, adrenaline, and serotonin firing the neurotransmitters in his brain like the night sky in July, and though they would be right to an extent, Peter imagined that in Greta's eyes he could sense the presence of something that had been so long absent in his life it was almost unrecognizable. Hope.

Early the next morning, he walked the four miles back to his sister's house rather than take a taxi. He was wide-awake, though he and Greta had stayed up most of the night talking.

Didier was in the kitchen, bare-chested under a striped silk robe, wearing espadrilles.

"*Ho!* The prodigal son returns," he said, pouring coffee through a ceramic dripper.

Lindsay came into the kitchen in bare feet, her long hair pulled back off her face. She rubbed her eyes with her right knuckle and squinted at him.

"You're back," she said.

He could tell that she was angry at him, though he wasn't exactly sure why.

Didier walked over to her and handed her a cup of coffee. He kissed her on the top of her head and then headed out into the garden with his copy of *Le Monde*. He motioned toward the empty coffee press to Peter on his way out.

"There is more coffee in the . . . *comment dit?*"

"Grinder." Both Peter and Lindsay spoke at the same time. Peter laughed. Even Didier couldn't annoy him today.

"Thanks Di Dawg," he said.

Didier let the screen door slam behind him.

Lindsay spoke without turning around. "Please don't call him that. He doesn't have the same sense of humor as you. He thinks you're being an asshole."

"Well, he wouldn't be the first," Peter said. He pulled himself up onto the kitchen counter and fiddled with the various wine and champagne corks scattered there. He picked one up and threw it at Lindsay. He aimed for her shoulder but caught her in the back of her head.

She whipped her chair around.

"What the fuck, Peter!"

"Why are you so angry with me? Are you still mad about the party? It was almost a week ago!"

"That party was for you," she said. "It was something nice I wanted to do for you, and you chose to go get high or whatever it was that you were doing."

He thought of telling her about Greta, but there was something in his sister's face that he hadn't seen since his arrival. All of the airiness of her party persona seemed to have vanished. There was a crease in between her eyebrows that he hadn't noticed the last time he saw her but that he instantly recognized. It was their mother's.

"I'm sorry," he said. He watched the back of her head as she stared at the computer screen in front of her, her shoulders slumping forward. And then she collapsed, burying her head in her arms.

Peter jumped down off the counter and studied the computer screen. His eyes scanned an e-mail from First Meridian Mortgage informing Lindsay Layton that she was being denied a loan. He looked at the other e-mails in her inbox and saw that the majority were from other banks and various mortgage companies.

"What's going on?" Peter asked.

Lindsay lifted her head up and opened her mouth to speak, but a sob caught in her throat and she started to cough instead. He waited for her to finish.

"I thought this one was going to come through. My financial adviser . . ." She trailed off and went back to her computer and started clicking through the e-mails.

"I have this one in here. Hang on, let me find it . . ." She opened one e-mail after the other. Peter looked at the top of the mail program and noticed that there were more than twenty-seven thousand e-mails in her inbox.

"How bad is it?" Peter asked, kneeling down next to her.

"I don't know, I can't tell," Lindsay said. "They said that they're going to foreclose on the house."

Peter put his hands on her shoulders and turned her away from the screen.

"Lindsay," he said. "Hey, Linds, look at me."

Lindsay lifted her eyes up to meet his. They had a wildness in them—her "crazy-eye" look, he had always called it. He recognized it from when they were little and their mother would drop them off at the ski area in the morning and tell them to stay on the intermediate blue runs; as soon as they scrambled out of their mother's Plymouth Voyager, Lindsay immediately headed for the black-diamond trails. She would always seek out the hill that was too steep, the drop that was too high, the turn too sharp. Before Lindsay would leap, she would give him the "crazy-eye" look. Peter knew even then that Lindsay was taking extraordinary chances with the singular hope that maybe this time would be the time that their father would come. He had already started a new family in Montreal with Joëlle, a French Canadian woman who had headed the language department at the university where their father had taught science. But by then, whether a birthday or a holiday, a fractured cheekbone or a slight concussion, nothing was ever enough to bring him back.

In the kitchen, Lindsay stared at him, sadness and fear mingling with fury. She needed Peter, just as she had once needed their father, and he could see in her expression that she couldn't help but resent her brother for that need.

"It'll be fine," she said. "It'll work out." She stood and began to tidy up, taking papers off the counter and idly placing them into little random piles by the stove. "So, where have you been going these nights?" she asked.

Peter hesitated and then told her about Greta.

Lindsay stopped and looked at her brother, surprise overriding the anxiety that had been giving her face that pinched look.

"Greta?" She looked confused. "You hooked up with Greta?"

Peter felt a twinge of annoyance and protectiveness.

"I didn't exactly hook up. I . . ." He stopped himself from trying to justify his feelings. "I like her." He settled on this understatement as a means to end the discussion. He didn't want to share this with anyone at this point. Not before he was sure of it. And not with Lindsay, who, from the time that they were in high school, had made a habit of becoming friends with whichever girl he was interested in. Before long that girl would be Lindsay's friend, and Peter would be relegated to the role of "Lindsay's brother." He stopped telling her about any woman he was interested in, even after he had moved to New York and the threat of Lindsay's interference had ended.

"Anyway, let's figure out what's going on with your finances," Peter said. "That's more pressing."

Lindsay shrugged and moved her attention to a bouquet of flowers, still wrapped in cellophane and stuck inside a champagne bucket. She took out a pair of scissors, unwrapped the flowers, and began cutting their stems under water.

"I just didn't picture you with Greta is all. Don't get me wrong. She's perfectly nice," Lindsay said, plucking the dead leaves off of the stems. She got a vase out of a low cupboard, filled it with water, and submerged the stems. "How old is she?" she asked.

"I don't know," Peter lied.

Lindsay looked up at him.

"Didn't come up," he said, lying again.

"She's got a kid, you know," Lindsay said. She took a penny from a dish full of change and tossed it into the vase. "And a husband. Though I guess right now they're separated?"

"Are you asking me?" Peter said. "Or telling me?"

"I'm sure you can take care of yourself." Lindsay flicked her hand out as though she were shooing away a bothersome insect, but Peter was relieved by the gesture. It meant she was extinguishing the subject for now.

Lindsay walked over to the window and watched Didier sitting in the sunlight, turning the pages of his paper. "Look at him," she said, gazing at Didier as though he were an exotic pet. Peter had seen the same expression on the faces of Persian cat breeders on nature programs.

"He really has a talent for living," she said.

"Does Didier know anything about the house being foreclosed upon?"

Lindsay shook her head. "He doesn't like to talk about money. He says that I'm obsessed with money and that I only talk about it to control him."

Peter thought of many different things to say, but knowing his sister's unfailing protectiveness toward Didier, he chose not to say anything.

"Lindsay, where is the money going? You have clients, right?"

"More than I can handle."

"And they pay you."

"Of course they pay me." She turned and looked at him. Their mother's crease reappeared between her eyebrows. "Why wouldn't they pay me?"

"I'm just trying to understand. Where is the money going? I mean, you don't have a family . . ."

Lindsay threw her hands up. "I don't know. I don't know where it goes, Peter. This house, everything in it. Didier's Hasselblads.

His office, my office. Salaries. The trips to Europe. The corridas in San Sebastian. The apartment he bought with his brother in Belleville. Didier's mother has needed help since she broke her hip, so we've been helping her . . . I don't know. It adds up."

"And does Didier pay for any of this?"

Lindsay shook her head.

"Do you even ask him to?"

"He said that he doesn't want this life. That it's only because of me." Lindsay opened a cupboard and took out a prescription bottle. She shook free a pill and then replaced the bottle in the cupboard.

"He said that he would be happy just to live in a suburb of Paris by himself eating pasta with ketchup, doing his art. He says that it's a sacrifice he makes to be with me."

As Lindsay poured herself a glass of water and swallowed the pill, Peter pictured Didier at the party, opening the bottles of wine and sniffing the corks.

Lindsay left the empty glass in the sink and walked back to the window. She put her hand up to the glass. Didier looked up from his paper, shielding his eyes from the sun. He smiled and blew her a kiss.

She turned back to Peter, her eyes full of tears and her chin trembling.

"And I don't want him to go away, Peter. I love him."

He felt alternately moved and revolted by his sister's devotion to this man, whom Peter had always dismissed as parasitical, preying on the generosity of his sister. But as he watched her gaze beatifically at him through the window, he noticed the color return to her face for the first time that morning. He had to consider that she wasn't only his for the taking, but that theirs was a mutually agreed upon symbiosis, one that had been evolving for a long time, until it was no longer clear who was the orchid or insect. It is undeniable that everyone in the world has a currency of some kind. His sister was beautiful, successful, and she loved him. And in return, Didier stayed, when many men before, beginning with the first one, had not—for this alone he was treasured.

Peter considered this, and the many other definitions of love and the many faces that it wears, during his remaining days in Los Angeles, spent mostly in the company of the woman he believed he had fallen in love with. He was still mulling over this question when Greta drove him to the airport to fly back to New York and retrieve his belongings. He and Greta had cautiously agreed to try and make a go of it and to eventually (possibly) introduce him to her six-year-old daughter in the coming months, depending on how their relationship progressed. He told Greta that he would leave it up to her and would see her as much or as little as she needed him. They both thought it best for Peter to stay with Lindsay until he found his own place.

At the entrance to airport security, Greta scrambled at the last minute to write all of her phone numbers and times that were good to call her, while Peter crouched down offering his back as a writing board. She impulsively kissed the paper and then, embarrassed, hurried to wipe away the light-pink lip print she had left before he wrestled it out of her hands, causing an uncharacteristic scene from two people who had tried for years, without even knowing they had been trying, to become invisible. She laughed and swatted him away as he grabbed and kissed her dramatically, bending her over backward as if they were ballroom dancing. As he gazed at her head drawn back, eyes squeezed tight in either terror or delight, the vein in her neck pulsing wildly, he thought of trying to exact a promise from her while he held her there, suspended. But he couldn't think of what. Promise you will love me? Promise you won't ever stop? And then the thought occurred to him that the moment you make someone promise anything is the same moment you ask them to lie to you. So he drew her up and set her back down on her feet. She looked at him with a question, and though every cell of him wanted to tell her that he loved her, another part of him, the part of him that used to play poker in college, told him that it was too early. And for the first time in years, he listened to that voice. So he kissed the inside of her hand, inhaling the vanishing scent of her skin, and turned away. As he entered the security line, he watched her standing there in the same place, like a beautiful tree. *Her hair turned into leaves, her arms into branches . . . her face lost in the canopy. Only her shining beauty was left.*

Every few steps he turned to look back at her, watching to see if she was still there. He removed his belt, his shoes, and anything that could be construed as a weapon and maneuvered his way unprotected through security.

WHEN IT HAPPENS TO YOU

WHEN IT HAPPENS TO YOU, you will be surprised. That thing they say about how you knew all the time but just weren't facing it? That might be the case, but nevertheless, there you will be. You will feel like you have been kicked in the stomach, that your insides have just separated to make room for something big.

You may not cry at first. You may wonder why you don't cry, and you may even feel like there is something seriously wrong with you. You might look at yourself as though you were a character in a book or a movie and you might think to yourself, "Why isn't that woman crying? What's wrong with her?"

It isn't the first time you will think that there is something wrong with you. You will search for the reason why he would choose her over you, why he would choose a girl over a woman. And then you will become certain that it is your age. You are spoiled—like the items in the pantry that were supposed to last indefinitely but somehow the pantry moths found their way inside. You will feel that you were thrown out just like that box of cereal was thrown out to keep everything else around it from becoming ruined.

If you are lucky enough to have children by then, you will struggle to explain to them why their parents no longer love each other the same way. Your children will assume that it is their fault, and though you will do your very best to explain to them why it isn't, a part of you will secretly fear that it is. You will have already looked at your children at times with a criti-cal eye and seen all of the youth and freshness that you and he once had, all that vitality and hope, and you will know that they took it away. You can't ever say that they stole it, because you gave it willingly. Still, once it was gone you missed it and envied it while hoping that you both would be strong enough to bear its absence.

He will not.

The girl who will give him back this illusion of vitality for a short time will not think of your children or your marriage. She will not consider the lovely years that you spent together with him. Why would she? She wasn't there when you both laughed your way through your wedding with a pure and nervous joy. She wasn't there when you both waited for your first child to be born. When he held your hand and told you how the contrac-tions were coming, with the seriousness of a boy, as he watched the peaks on the machine that was connected to your belly—you listening to the wondrous familiarity of his voice as though all of your lives depended on it, though truthfully your body knew already in the moments before. She wasn't there when you held him upright at his father's funeral and then at his mother's only weeks after. Or for the vacations, alone at first and then with the children. Or the holidays, alternating between your family and his, while they were still alive, then later with just your own. The notes you composed together to the tooth fairy. The nights you stayed up talking, even though you had to work the next day, and held hands as you fell asleep hoping to have the same dream.

When it happens to you, you will ask him why he would choose to forsake this good, sweet life that you carefully built together for a girl who couldn't begin to understand him. And then you will realize that that is at least partially the point. He doesn't want to be understood. He wants to be misunderstood because in that misunderstanding lies the possibility of reinvention.

When it happens to you, you will wonder if he loved her. He will assure you that he did not, that it wasn't about love. He will tell you that it was about something else entirely. But even in your quietest moments together, he will be unable to specify what that something else was. He will honestly seem as confused as you, even to the point of bewilderment.

After it happens, you will hear the girl's name everywhere. It will seem that every baby born that year will carry her name.

Of course, you will be reminded that there are worse things. Far worse. Your children are healthy, you will tell yourself. Neither you nor anyone that you know has cancer, for example. That would be a real tragedy. A journalist you will hear on the radio will talk about how he wasn't allowed to use the word "tragedy" in an article he wrote as it pertained to an artist, a man who had died in his fifties. One can't use that word, he was told by the editors of the national paper. Not when there is genocide in the world. Not as long as ethnic cleansing exists, and landmines. And rape. And that's not even taking into account the natural disasters—earthquakes and tsunamis. Floods. Levees that don't hold. Whole towns that are washed away. Children who are left without parents, or worse, parents who are left without their children. These are occurrences from which the heart does not recover. These are tragedies.

And yet you will find that when it happens to you, your heart won't listen to reason. Because for all the wisdom you will have accumulated up to that point, in all the years you have been alive, your heart is just a muscle like any other. Full of blood and veins, hungry for oxygen. Your heart doesn't think. Your heart is stupid. It doesn't consider the relativity of tragedy when it breaks.

You will ask him for details, and reluctantly he will give them to you. But no matter how many he gives, it will never seem to reach critical mass. You will want to know more. You should know that even one detail is too much, but you will think (mistakenly, of course) that if you know them all it will make it less special. That in the retelling it will seem banal or even sordid.

And so he tells you.

You will find out that one day, when it first began, they had sex more than once. You will know the color of her pubic hair, the little that she had left after waxing. He will tell you how she played Mozart on the violin in bed before they put their clothes back on, and how he openly cried in front of her while she played. He will tell you that she orgasmed through intercourse. He will tell you this, knowing that it is something that you tried and failed your entire life to accomplish, but he will only do so under duress. Your hands will be balled into little shaking fists at your side as you threaten to strike him unless he answers, and yes, he could lie to you, but he will have had enough of lying by then. You both will have had enough of it.

Any sane person will tell you that these are details that you don't need to have, but there again, the stupid heart doesn't listen.

When it happens to you, you think that you might die. You won't. This isn't the kind of thing that you die from, but at night when you can't sleep from all of these details that keep you from resting and you're gasping for air, you'll wish that you would die. You'll wish that it would happen by accident so that your children won't have to live wondering why you would ever do such a thing. During the worst nights, you will find yourself plotting.

And then one day, you'll stop.

And when you look in your children's bright faces in the daylight, you will feel shame that you could ever have considered it and still call yourself a mother.

And then you will cry. And then you won't stop crying. You will turn to him for comfort because you won't know where else to turn. There is no one else who knows the intricacy of your pain. And he will bear it because he has to.

You will try everything to heal yourself. You will take drugs prescribed by doctors. You'll take drugs *not* prescribed by doctors. You will find yourself praying, though you stopped believing in God a long time ago. No matter, you will start praying like you were taught to do when you were a child. You will even get down on your hands and knees to do it.

You will go to therapy and strive to find your part in it. Your complicity. You will nod when the therapist tells you that if you do the work, you can have the marriage you always dreamed of. But I *had* the marriage I always dreamed of, you'll tell her. No, she will assure you. You only *thought* you did. You will try to make sense of this "hall of mirrors" way of looking at your life. Mostly, you will just miss the marriage that you had but didn't have.

And then, if you haven't already, you will look at yourself closely to see if there was something you did in your life that made you deserve this. And when you do, chances are you will think of me.

When it happens to you, you may wonder if after all this time you were forgiven.

Ask me then, Theresa, and I will try to answer.

THE LITTLE ONE

BETTY LOOKED OUT HER WINDOW and there again was the girl. She was hidden, or at least attempting to hide, but Betty could clearly see her curly white-blond hair sticking out of the overgrown rosemary bush that Harry had planted years ago, in between relapses. What was she doing in there? Waiting for her? She thought of coming out on the porch and calling out to the girl, inviting her in to play on the out-of-tune piano or to look through the old encyclopedias, but the thought of entertaining the six-year-old now frightened her. She backed away from the window and stalled by making herself a pot of chamomile tea. By the time the tea finished brewing, she told herself, she would go out and deal with the child. Explain to her, yet again, the rules that she must learn to abide by if she is to enter into someone's home. Rules that her own parents should have taught the girl themselves but obviously hadn't.

Not to say that Betty herself was a model mother. She wasn't, as her own daughter, Mandy, from whom she has been more or less estranged for the last twenty years, reminded her whenever reconciliation was attempted. When Harry came out of remission for the last time, though they both would have preferred the peace that surely would have prevailed had they neglected to inform their only daughter, Harry convinced her that it would be far worse for Betty once he was gone if they shut Mandy out of this last all-important moment. Give her a chance to say good-bye to her father—the man she had antagonized her entire life in a misguided attempt to force him to prove he loved her.

Betty shuffled from the stove to the butcher-block island with the teakettle. With her good hand, she poured the steaming water over the loose chamomile leaves into the Hable teapot that she and Harry had bought in Sausalito after they married, back in 1959. They were both grad students at Berkeley then, where they would stay through all of the demonstrations and riots and then fall with embarrassing comfort into teaching positions for the next twenty years, amidst the atmosphere of chaos and revolution swirling around them. The politics were a part of life, and Harry and Betty managed to lean to the left without ever getting sucked into it. It was a romantic, tumultuous background to their own love story, but neither wanted to commit much time to politics. The world was changing from the one they had known as children, and yet Harry and Betty felt that the boldest and most daring, the most downright countercultural statement they could make was to love only each other. And that is what they did. And then, despite the great pains they had taken to not get pregnant, Mandy was born in the latter half of the sixties, and everything changed.

Now it had been almost seven years since Harry had been gone. Dead. She should be able to say that word, Betty knew, but it still got stuck in her throat. She still found herself, when forced to have conversations with people—admittedly few now that she had retired from her teaching position at UCLA— talking about him as though he were still there. She reminded herself each time she began a conversation to say, "My late husband," but couldn't quite get out the word "late." "Late." What did this word mean in this context, and why should she connect this word to Harry, who was never late once in his life? Harry was early for everything—classes, parties, funerals. He was early to the point where it verged on the hostile, as one of their old Berkeley friends, Joyce, used to say. And my "dead" husband was out of the question. So he just remained Harry— "my husband, Harry"—whom he had been for nearly all of Betty's life, and with a determination that her daughter Mandy dismissed as "mulish," that's what he would remain.

Betty went to the cupboard and took out two cups and sau-cers and set them next to the teapot. Seven years was enough time to stop this nonsense and she knew it, but the anxiety that she felt pouring just the one cup for herself was far greater than the knowledge that she was just a little "touched"—not to mention the waste of it. When people were there, she managed not to pour Harry's cup or to fix Harry's plate, but when alone, as she was now, and there was no one there to comment, she gave in to her weakness. But as she filled the two cups, side by side, she could see Mandy in her mind's eye shaking her head at her, with an expression that said, "Mother. Get a hold of yourself."

The first time she met the girl, Betty was out in the yard trimming the camellias. The girl had just returned home from grocery shopping with her mother, and while the trunk was being unloaded, the girl raced into the little plot of land that separated the two properties and climbed the tree.

"Not too high, Charlotte," her mother called out to her as she toted the bags of groceries from her car into the house. She waved to Betty, and though she and the girl's mother had never spoken, Betty waved back.

She went back to her pruning, carefully cutting on the angles above the buds. It took her much longer than it used to take since she had to use her good hand, which was not the dominant one. The doctors had failed to find exactly what it was that ailed her; carpal tunnel, arthritis, Ulnar Nerve Entrapment—it was diagnosed as all of these at one time or another, but no one could explain why it affected only the one hand. She eventually just gave up on the drugs—they never seemed to work anyway—and concentrated on becoming ambidextrous at age seventy-two.

"I like your hat."

Betty looked up and saw the girl's legs dangling from the tree.

"Were you speaking to me?" Betty asked.

"You're wearing a hat, aren't you?" the girl said. Her tone contained exasperation but no malice.

"Why, yes I am," Betty said. "You have very good powers of observation."

The girl jumped down out of the tree and sidled over to the edge of Betty's property.

"What's oversation?" she asked, mispronouncing the word.

"Ob-ser-va-tion," Betty said, enunciating each syllable. "It comes from the word 'observe'—to notice, to see things. I just told you that you are good at seeing things."

The girl shifted her weight from one skinny leg to the other.

"It's just a hat," she said.

Betty reached up and touched the brim and smiled at the girl. "It's a very special hat, you know."

The girl leaned forward, curious.

"What's special about it? What's it do?"

"It's special," Betty said, "because Harry gave it to me."

"Who's Harry?"

"Harry is my husband. He gave me this hat many, many years ago, probably before you were even born."

"I'm six. Almost seven," the girl said, scratching a bug bite on her leg.

Almost seven, Betty remarked to herself with disbelief. Most likely, this girl was growing in her mother's uterus as the cancer was growing and ravaging Harry's body. Betty tried to distract herself from the grim, morbid thought by removing the brown leaves from the plant so that only the glossy green ones remained.

The girl found a stick and poked at the pieces of bark she was standing on. "So how would you say . . ." she began, "like for example, if I was good at doing what other people wanted to do instead of just what I wanted to do, you'd say I'm *flexible*—"

"Are you flexible?" Betty asked, looking up.

The girl frowned. "I wasn't finished. But no. I'm not. Louisa and Rose are flexible. I'm *organized*." She puffed out her chest, creating a distinct *C* curve in her back and belly that seemed incongruous with the rest of her. "That means you keep things in order, and everyone says that I do that the best out of everyone."

"You look organized," Betty said.

"It isn't really something you can tell by looking," the girl said. "But what I wanted to know was, if I was good at that word you said . . ."

"Observation," Betty said

"Yeah, if I'm good at that . . ."

"Then you would be observant."

"Oh." The girl ran back to the tree and grabbed one of its lower branches and swung her legs up onto it. She hung upside down from the branch, her hair tumbling in long blond curls toward the ground.

"Did you and Harry get divorced?" she asked.

Betty shook her head. "No. We are not divorced," she said. She considered telling the rest of it, but the girl's curiosity seemed satisfied, and Betty told herself that she could explain it next time. It was a ruse that she often used with herself—the putting off till the next time, and then the next, until the awkwardness of telling became too great and she could rest permanently in the solace of omission. Betty went back to her trimming and hummed a Locatelli sonata that she had been listening to on the radio earlier that morning.

"Charlotte!" The girl's mother's voice carried down the hill.

The girl reached up and took hold of the branch with her hands and then fell to the ground. She ran home to her mother without saying good-bye.

And so began the daily and sometimes twice-daily visits from the young girl. She would show up unexpectedly, linger for a few minutes, and leave with just as little notice. There were some days when Betty would return from running errands, usually the post office or the grocery store, to find some sort of talisman of the girl's having come to visit. A pile of sticks carefully arranged just outside the front door or a small bouquet of flowers torn from Betty's own garden. After a couple of these makeshift bouquets, Betty felt obliged to ask the girl not to pick flowers from the garden but to leave the blossoms intact for other people to appreciate. Betty hadn't even finished the sentence before the girl's cheeks reddened and she raced home in silent fury.

She didn't see her for a few days after that, and Betty was surprised to find that in spite of all the years that she had felt trapped when in the company of Mandy, her own flesh and blood, for some inexplicable reason she missed the girl's presence. She was confounded by the familiar stab of loss connected to this tiny stranger, and just when she had resigned herself to bear yet another absence, the girl reappeared. Betty was so overjoyed to see the girl sitting outside her front door that she wept—an uncharacteristic display that shocked her. She told the girl it was hay fever.

A couple of days later, Betty was at her desk, attempting to get through a large pile of bills that she had been putting off for too long, when she heard strains of a violin coming from outside. She recognized it as "La Cinquantaine" by Gabriel-Marie. When she opened the door, the girl was sitting on her porch with a small violin tucked underneath her chin, playing the song remarkably well. When she had finished, she looked up at Betty and grinned.

"I bet you didn't know that I could play violin, did you?" she said.

Betty sat down on the wicker chair next to the door. "I certainly did not," she said. "You are full of surprises."

"I used to take violin lessons twice a week, since I was three," the girl said. "That's almost . . . hang on." She paused, puzzling through the math in her head. "Four years ago."

"And you don't take violin lessons anymore? That's a shame, you play so beautifully."

"My last teacher moved away," the girl said. She took her bow and brushed a curl off her forehead with the tip of it. "My mommy said that she would find me a new teacher, but then she doesn't."

"Well, you tell your mother to hurry up and find a new teacher."

"You can tell her yourself. She's just next door. She's not doing anything."

Betty smiled and shook her head. "You tell her for me. I have to get back to paying my bills now."

"Do you have a lot of money?"

"That's not an appropriate question, you know," Betty said.

"Why not?" the girl asked. "I have a lot of money. I put two dollars in my bank account every week, plus the birthday money that my oma and opa send me, and my mommy says that when I'm a teenager, if I keep saving, I'll have enough money to buy a car."

Betty stood up and smoothed out the creases of her khaki slacks.

"Well, I wish you the very best with that. Please excuse me now while I finish paying my bills." She patted the soft bed of curls on the girl's head and turned to go back in her house.

"How's Harry?" the girl asked.

Betty's stomach lurched at the sound of her husband's name in the voice of someone else. She stopped in midstep, struggling to maintain her balance, and sat down quickly. Touching her hand to her forehead, she patted away the perspiration.

"He's very well," Betty said after a moment. "Thank you for asking."

The girl smiled and lifted her violin back onto her shoulder.

"Can I play you my song again before you go inside?"

"Yes, dear," Betty said. "Play it for me once more."

She leaned back in the wicker chair. Closing her eyes, she recalled the summer nights in Berkeley when she and Harry would picnic together during the season of open-air concerts, Mandy sleeping next to them in a Moses basket. It was a time when, unlike their peers who longed for the catharsis of a Monterey Festival or a Woodstock, she and Harry had shared a passion only for classical music. Mozart. Vivaldi. Chopin. Chamber music. Opera. Harry used to say that long ago if there was a soundtrack to their life together, it would be Glenn Gould playing the Goldberg Variations—they made a point of seeing him every chance they had until he no longer performed in public. Many years had passed since Betty had heard any music live, and listening to the girl play the violin for her now swept Betty back to those days, which felt both sweet and savage in the remembering.

Before long, the girl managed to further weave herself into the fabric of Betty's life. It was during a stretch of unseasonable summer rain when Betty, on impulse, invited the girl into the house. As she wandered through the living room, she made a point of touching everything with her index finger extended like a conductor's baton. Then she stopped at a framed piece of faded collage art that an old student had made for Harry back in the seventies. The student had been a sullen girl with long, truly black hair—apparently due to some Native American blood—parted down the middle, as was the fashion back then, gathering into dark, inky pools on her shoulders. The student admired Harry to the point of distraction, and although he would never dare to admit temptation, he judiciously introduced the student to Betty early on in the semester, defusing whatever intriguing ambiguity may or may not have existed. Betty became a mentor to the young woman and had her in her linguistics class the following year. She still received a Christmas card from the woman every year, addressed by hand.

"We love life, not because we are used to living but because we are used to loving."

—FRIEDRICH NIETZSCHE

The girl read the quote from the collage aloud, mispronouncing Nietzsche's name.

Betty corrected her.

"Nee-chuh? He has a funny name," the girl said.

"It's German," Betty told her. "That's Harry's, you know. A student of his made it for him years ago, and he is very fond of it."

She was acutely aware of only using the present tense, and for a moment, Betty was seized by a nagging guilt at the thought of deliberately deceiving someone—a child, no less. But the luxurious relief of allowing herself to speak freely of her husband was ultimately greater than the uncomfortable ethical dilemma. Time is a fluid thing for children anyway, she told herself. She remembered when Mandy was a little girl and how she would tell stories of events as though they had happened years earlier, when in truth only a week or two had passed. *Time doesn't exist, but things go to the feeling of time.* Which philosopher was responsible for that one? How she missed calling out to Harry and hearing him always supply the correct answer.

"Did all of his students have funny names?" the girl asked.

Betty laughed. "No, dear. Nietzsche didn't make that for him. He was just the person who said it. He was a philosopher. That is what Harry taught, philosophy."

As Betty said this word, she mentally prepared herself to define it, but the girl didn't ask. She continued strolling around the room, eyeing artifacts like a conscientious shopper, until she arrived at the bookshelf. She sat down in front of it cross-legged and reached for a book from the bottom shelf. Betty cleared her throat.

Abruptly, the girl stopped and looked over to Betty for permission.

"Go ahead," Betty told her. "Just be careful."

"Can I have a glass of milk?" the girl asked.

"Is that how we ask for things?" Betty said.

"Can I *please* have a . . . stupid glass of milk?" she said.

"No you may not," Betty said. "Not until you ask nicely. And we don't say *can*. We say *may*."

The girl narrowed her eyes into slits and jutted out her chin. She took a deep breath and held it for a moment. Then she let out the air through slightly puckered lips. It was an affectation, and Betty wondered if she had acquired it from her mother.

"May I please, please, *please* have a glass of milk?"

Betty nodded and went into the kitchen, fetching a glass from the cupboard. She had milk in her refrigerator only by chance. Normally, she drank her morning tea with half-and-half, but since it was coming up on what would have been their fifty-second wedding anniversary, Betty had bought milk to prepare his favorite dish: New England clam chowder, from a recipe Harry's mother gave to Betty before they eloped. It was the only thing that Harry's mother had ever given her. The taciturn New Englander blamed Betty for the elopement, and the subsequent relocation further cemented her rancor toward the eighteen-year-old Betty. No matter how many times Harry warned his mother, she never stopped insulting his young bride. In their first year of marriage, Harry made the choice to sever ties with her, the mother with whom he had shared a great affinity throughout his childhood and adolescence. Their relationship never recovered, even after Betty herself begged Harry to reconcile in the years after his mother was diagnosed with the same cancer that would one day claim his own life. It was one of the few things that Harry remained inflexible about, and though Betty would have preferred not to have been the source of familial discord, she couldn't deny the thrill of being so rapturously regarded by one's own husband. Though he never had any more contact with his mother, at the height of her teenage rebellion Mandy sought out the woman and forged a bond. As a result, Mandy inherited most of the estate—along with Harry's older sister, Janet, a spinster. Not that there was much to inherit, and what Mandy did receive she squandered.

On what? wondered Betty. Probably drugs or an interminable list of inappropriate men.

Betty walked back into the living room holding the glass of milk with her good hand, trying not to spill, and found the girl gone. The encyclopedia lay on the floor, open to a page on the Superb Fairy-Wren—an Australian bird noted for its social monogamy and sexual promiscuity. Betty closed the book and placed it back on the shelf.

Once school vacation began, the girl began to linger for longer stretches of time. They worked together side by side in the garden, where the girl proved herself to be a diligent helper, and on wet and gloomy days, she lay down on the braided rug in the center of the living room with one of the encyclopedias while Betty read or sorted through mail. Their discourse was easy and Betty welcomed the childish queries about Harry. What is his favorite color? (Green.) Does he know how to fly a plane? (No.) Did he ever have a pet guinea pig? (No.) The girl seemed to accept his physical absence as though one might an imaginary friend, and her questions gave Betty the opportunity to savor her time with Harry. She told long, sprawling anecdotes about the first time that she and Harry met at a county fair in western Massachusetts. The time that Harry discovered that she wasn't ironing his shirts but buying them in bulk from JCPenney while stashing the soiled shirts behind the freezer in the garage.

"Why didn't you tell him the truth?" the girl asked. "My

mommy tells me that if you always tell the truth you won't get into trouble."

"Your mother is correct," Betty said. "I didn't tell him the truth because I was embarrassed. I wanted him to think I was perfect."

"My teacher at school says that there is no such thing as perfect. And if you can't make mistakes, you can't make anything."

"Well, you have some very intelligent people around you."

"But I like to be perfect, too," the girl said, after a moment of thought. "I threw my violin away 'cause I couldn't make the song perfect."

"Perfection is the enemy of the good," Betty said, turning over an *Atlantic Monthly* magazine subscription renewal form addressed to Harry D. Arthur. She set it aside onto his pile.

"I hate the violin," the girl said.

"Oh no, but you play so beautifully!"

The girl shook her head violently and turned over on her back attempting a backbend. The blood rushed to her already-flushed face as she strained to stay in the position.

"My mommy doesn't like the violin."

Betty was puzzled. Why would she sign her own daughter up for years of violin lessons if she didn't like it? Clearly the girl had talent, but there must be more to the story. Betty had forgotten how you only get slivers of stories from children—usually what they echo from overheard adult conversations.

The girl fell back on the rug and reached her arms up, grabbed her ankles and rocked back and forth.

"Did Harry ever . . . live somewhere else?" the girl asked.

"Live somewhere else, you mean before we met?"

"No," she said. "I mean, did you ever decide that maybe you would live with someone else—even though you still loved him?"

Betty looked at the girl's face, reading the anxiety and confusion in it. She paused as she considered how to answer.

"Never mind, I don't care," the girl said.

"No, dear. Harry and I never tried that—though there are many married people who do. Sometimes . . . it can be a way to have clarity. To see things more clearly."

"My mommy would rather be with someone who plays with a polar bear instead of my daddy." Her face crumpled and tears slid down the side of her cheeks. "It's not even a *real* polar bear. It's for babies. A stupid show for stupid babies."

She turned over onto her stomach and hid her face in her arms. Betty watched the girl's shoulders shake, though no sound emerged.

Betty struggled to kneel beside the girl. She patted her small back and stroked her hair.

"I'm sorry, dear."

The girl sat upright and turned to face Betty, her lashes clumped together with the wetness. Betty was struck by how much she resembled a doll that Mandy had played with when little. The doll had been her constant companion for years until she left it on a train when the three of them went to Europe for the first and only time as a family.

"Whenever I ask my daddy who he loves more, me or

Mommy, he says that Mommy is the heart and I'm the heart inside the heart." The girl wiped her nose with the back of her hand and dried it on the front of her pinafore sundress. She began to cry again even harder.

"Your daddy sounds very sweet," Betty said softly.

"But that means when he doesn't love Mommy anymore, he won't love me anymore because I'm inside Mommy's heart!"

She threw herself against Betty, pressing her face against her soft midsection.

"No, he will always love you." Even as she spoke these banal words of reassurance, Betty was reminded that she herself was living proof that it was possible to fall out of love with your child. The pull of parental love had been tenuous for both her and Harry from the very beginning—and it hadn't taken all that much for it to give out entirely. Perhaps there is a finite amount of love that we are all allotted, Betty thought to herself, and Harry took it all, just as she took his, and there was simply nothing left for their child. Mandy should have been an enhancement, that is what one's children were supposed to be, but instead she was an obstacle. They didn't know how to talk to her or how to be with her, and they both viewed her as a rival in a contest that she had little chance of winning. As hard as it was to admit, even all these years later, it wasn't Mandy's fault how things had turned out. "You made me who I am!" Mandy would scream at Betty when she was a teenager, as incident after incident piled up—failing grades, school suspensions, car accidents. And then, into her twenties, the apartment evictions, the job firings—not to mention the readily available drugs that were so hard for Mandy to resist, in even the best of circumstances. "If you and Daddy could have deigned to share some of your precious love with me, maybe I wouldn't have grown up to be such a fuck-up."

There was no point in arguing. Betty knew that Mandy was right, and there was nothing to be gained in making Mandy feel crazy in addition to unloved. All Betty could do was apologize and tell her daughter that she deserved more.

Holding the girl in her arms like this now made Betty shudder as she considered how her own daughter might react had she been watching. At forty-four years old, Mandy—or Amanda, as she now insisted on being called—had enjoyed little success in her chosen career as an artist and even less in matters of the heart. All of this only seemed like further proof that as much as she had excelled as a wife, Betty's failure as a mother was exponential in comparison.

"I love you," she heard the girl's muffled voice say. The weight of the ensuing silence seemed to take the air from the room.

"I love you, too," Betty said aloud, without even thinking. She felt the girl sigh as her body relaxed against her own. Hearing herself say the three words that had always been reserved for just one person was both pleasant and unexpected.

She was most surprised to discover that she meant it.

Rosella, the Guatemalan cleaning woman who came once a week to help with the deep cleaning and laundry, asked Betty if it would be okay to bring along her eight-year-old daughter now that school was out for the summer. Betty told Rosella that it was fine, and for the first couple of weeks the woman's daughter sat at the kitchen table without incident, reading books and coloring while her mother cleaned. Rosella spoke little English, and if her daughter had more facility with the language, her shyness kept her from revealing it. Betty smiled at her and offered some of the sugar-free hard candy that she had purchased for the girl, but mostly Betty tried to stay out of the way until Rosella was finished.

Betty hadn't seen the girl for a couple of weeks. During the last visit, the girl had mentioned something about going to Washington state to visit with her grandparents, so Betty assumed that was where the girl was. Betty missed her and looked forward to the girl's return. The help in the garden, the impromptu concerts, but most of all the conversations about Harry. Having the girl gone revealed to Betty just how accustomed she had become to the company. She had begun to crave it, and some days she found herself standing by the window, as though she were a maiden waiting for her beloved to appear galloping over the mountain.

She was in the kitchen sorting through a drawer of mismatched Tupperware when she heard the girl's footsteps padding up the gravel path.

"Betttyyyy!" the girl's voice rang out, bright and impatient as a nest of newborn starlings. Betty stood up a little too fast, leaving the drawer open, and hurried past Rosella's daughter, who sat quietly on the couch reading a Judy Moody book in

Spanish while her mother finished up her cleaning in the bathroom.

Betty threw the door open and groaned as the girl collided into her with the force of a bullet. She threw herself at Betty and circled her midsection with her tiny slender arms.

Betty laughed and stroked the girl's head. "There she is!"

"Did you miss me?" the girl asked. "Did you wonder where I was? Did you think I got took by robbers?"

Betty's eyes burned with emotion. She discreetly wiped the corners with her pinky.

"I did not think you were taken by robbers," she said. "I would never think such a thing."

She held the girl's hand, and together they walked into the house.

"But robbers take kids like me all the time," the girl insisted with a pout. "My daddy says never to talk to strangers 'cause they might really be a robber."

"Your daddy is absolutely correct, and you should listen to him, but you told me that you were going to visit your grandparents. . . ."

Betty stopped talking as she took notice of the girl standing frozen in place. She was staring at Rosella's daughter on the couch, squinting with an immediate and visceral dislike. She dropped Betty's hand.

"Girls," Betty began tentatively, "let me introduce . . ." But before she had the opportunity to say anything more, the girl ran out of the house, slamming the screen door behind her. Rosella's daughter stared up at Betty with large, frightened eyes, sensing that she was somehow responsible for the girl's sudden departure.

Betty emerged from the house just in time to witness the girl decapitating the last of her Dahlias. She hurled the deep-red oversized flowers in a pile and stomped on them with fury.

"Young lady!" Betty called out to her. "Just what do you think you are doing?"

The girl ignored her and kicked the pile with her small sandaled foot.

"You stop that right now!" Betty hobbled down the steps and made her way to where the girl stood glaring at Betty with her hands balled into little fists by her side.

"Are you going to tell Harry?" the girl asked. There was a glint in her eye that Betty had not seen before. "Are you?"

Betty's breath became short, and she brought her hand up to her chest. She held it there, feeling the frenzied rhythm of her heart.

The girl's eyelids lowered halfway as she stared up at Betty with a coldness that reminded Betty of a carved marble statue perched atop a grave.

"He's dead," the girl said.

It was cruel, and it was true, and Betty felt something inside of her break into tiny sharp pieces. She staggered backward in stunned silence.

"He's dead and you just *pretend* that he's here."

When Betty finally found her voice, it was because she was screaming.

"Get out!"

She did not stop screaming even after the girl had fled for the refuge of her own home, in search of her mother's arms.

Betty had no idea how she had ended up in the hospital. She woke to find a Hispanic male nurse checking her vital signs. When asked, he cheerfully explained that her housekeeper had heard screaming; when she ran outside to see what was happening, Rosella found Betty unconscious on the driveway.

Betty looked down and felt the thin hospital gown she was wearing. She lifted her head off the pillow and felt it throb.

"You lay back, girl. You ain't going nowhere tonight."

"Where are my clothes?" Betty asked.

"We got 'em, don't you worry. You just rest your pretty head and I'll let the doctor know you're awake. Okay?"

Betty took a deep breath to temper the anger she could feel rising. She was seventy-three years old, with a lifetime of experience and wisdom and pain, and yet with each passing year, more and more people spoke to her as though she were a child. The indignity of being condescended to by people a third of her age made her want to howl with rage. "Just snub 'em, Betts," Harry used to say to her with his smile. "We used to be that smart, remember?"

The nurse gathered up his supplies, and as he drew the curtain back, Betty was horrified to see a body lying in the bed adjacent to hers. The patient's face was shriveled and gray and put Betty in mind of a trophy on a headhunter's stick. If she hadn't seen the chest moving up and down, Betty would have been sure the woman was dead. Turning her head away from the sight in revulsion, Betty stared up at the darkening sky visible through the tiny window.

"Your daughter says she be back after she go get something to eat," the nurse said on his way out. "Okay now? You just rest."

"My daughter?" Betty lifted her head again, but the man disappeared on his rounds, whistling. Surely he must have been mistaken. Betty hadn't spoken to Mandy in years—she probably didn't even have a recent number. When Betty tried to conjure up an image of her daughter, she could only recall her as a teenager, just before she and Harry decided to send her back east to boarding school. Her beautiful dark hair had been bleached so many times that it practically disintegrated if she ran a brush through it, which she rarely did. And her eyes were caked with so much makeup that Betty wondered how Mandy could even see through the curtain of mascara. She remembered all of the mascara running down Mandy's face as she begged not to be sent away. That night Betty dreamed that her daughter had been killed in a plane crash, and they woke up to find that Mandy never made it to school—she ran away upon arriving at Logan Airport. She turned up at Harry's mother's in Maine, where she remained for the rest of her high school years. Her mother-in-law would send Harry pictures from time to time and they couldn't help but notice how much better Mandy looked: her hair short and dark, her body lanky and strong. It was as if the old woman was taunting Betty with every image. "This is what you couldn't do," she seemed to be saying. Betty closed her eyes and tried to push away the regret. When she opened them again, it was Mandy's face that stared down at her.

"Hi, Mom."

Betty blinked at her, unsure if she was still dreaming. She tried to sit up and noticed for the first time that she was attached to an IV.

"Don't sit up. Just rest."

"I don't understand," Betty said. "How did you . . ."

"Your neighbor found an old number in your phone book," Mandy said. "Luckily, I rented my old apartment to a . . . friend, and she called me." Betty noticed the way her daughter hesitated when she said the word "friend," understanding that she was more than a friend.

Mandy looked good. Better than she had years ago when Harry was sick. Her dark hair had a few gray strands running through it, but her face was more relaxed than Betty could remember ever seeing it. "I talked to the doctor and helped them sort out your insurance information," she said.

"The doctor was supposed to come speak to me. Why didn't he come speak to me?"

Mandy reached out and touched her on the arm. "He will, Mom. Don't worry. You're fine. You just took a fall, and they want to rule out seizures or stroke."

She smiled at Betty as though to offer reassurance, but then her eyes filled with tears. Mandy rummaged in her bag until she found a tissue. "It seems that you were upset about something before you took the fall, or that's what your housekeeper was trying to tell your neighbor," Mandy said. "I didn't get the full story, third-hand, you know."

Betty shifted in the bed at the thought of the girl kicking the pile of Dahlias across the yard.

"Did something happen?" asked Mandy, leaning forward.

The girl's face came into Betty's mind as her expression changed from fury to fear when Betty screamed at her.

She shook her head. "I don't remember."

Mandy nodded and ran her hand through her hair. Betty noticed a thin gold band on her ring finger.

"You know, Mom, I've been meaning to call you. I dialed your number so many times. . . ."

She seemed to be waiting for Betty to say something. When Betty didn't speak, Mandy continued, though her voice sounded as if it had lost some confidence.

"I know that it wasn't so"—she took a deep breath, searching for the right word—"peaceful. When Daddy died."

Betty closed her eyes to refrain from commenting on Mandy's understatement.

"But I want you to know . . . that I'm happier now." She looked at Betty and Betty saw Harry's eyes looking back at her. She had never realized how much father and daughter resembled each other. Like Harry, Mandy's irises were the color of polished maple, and with age she had acquired the same wrinkles finely etched around the sides. It gave her face a softer look, almost maternal.

"I'm pleased," Betty said.

Mandy laughed a great big guttural laugh. "Well, I'm pleased you're pleased, Mom. I really am."

Betty heard the opening bars of the Goldberg Variations. Abruptly, Mandy reached for her enormous handbag. She withdrew a cell phone and answered. "Hi," she said, with a secret smile on her face. "I'm at the hospital. Fine, fine." She half turned away from Betty as she spoke to the person on the line, from her tone obviously an intimate acquaintance. Betty observed how her daughter kept her answers short (yes, yes, no) so that Betty would not be able to ascertain the content of the conversation. It was a strategy that she and Harry had often used when Mandy was in the room. That and speaking Latin (*O pro poena ut subsisto*).

When Mandy hung up the phone, she sat down on the chair beside the bed and looked at Betty. Then she laughed and threw her head back with a groan. It was an exasperated noise that expressed everything she was unable to articulate with words, a lifetime of the stifled conversation between mother and daughter.

"Stop it," Betty said. "You'll wake the dead," she added, jerking her head toward the neighboring bed. She meant it to be funny, but the word "dead" spooked her. It was lurking everywhere now, behind every corner. In every conversation. In the evening news, every reunion with old friends—it seemed always that someone was dying. Soon, very soon, Betty knew, it would be her. If she were a religious woman, she would have been comforted by this fact. She would have suffered through any illness gladly, no matter how long and protracted—cancer, dementia, all of the insults of old age—if she could only do so with the assurances of being reunited with Harry. But she was not a believer, and as much as she longed for the comfort of an afterlife with Harry, where she would be joyfully reunited with her beloved, she knew that this was not, could not be so. The moment the light went out of Harry's eyes, he was gone forever. The room went cold. And if she was to survive in this world, she would have to learn to live with that shift in temperature.

Betty drifted to sleep that night with Mandy seated silently beside her. In the morning, the hospital discharged Betty and she sat in the passenger seat of Mandy's hybrid car while her daughter drove carefully, under the speed limit, minding all of the safety signals, as if to show her mother how she had grown up. Together, they tentatively began the long, arduous process of stitching together the remnants of what remained. Betty leaned her head against the seat and gazed at the familiarity of Harry's face in her daughter's profile.

She's all that's left of him, she thought. The blood of my own. The first little one.

Betty brought the cup of tea to her lips and realized that it had gone cold. Yet another example of the fractious and intractable properties of time and how it accelerates with age. She imagined the impatience of the girl in the rosemary bush and wondered if she was still there at all. A quick glance out the window answered her question. The girl was still there, only now she was seated cross-legged, peering up at the house with a look of stubborn hopefulness on her face.

In a few hours, Mandy would be picking her up to take her to the hospital for some bothersome follow-up tests, but for now Betty's time belonged to her, to do with as she pleased. She put the kettle on again and walked to the sink, staring for a moment into the mystery of the drain. She could feel the heat of the sun coming through the window. Lifting Harry's cup, she watched the trickle of liquid fall into its depth. She washed the cup carefully, dried it with a dishtowel, and placed it face-down back in the cupboard.

And then Betty walked to the door, opened it wide, and let the girl in.

MEA CULPA

PHILLIP HAD LOVED THREE WOMEN in his life and had betrayed every one of them. This was noted with interest by his new therapist, Gerald, a man he guessed to be maybe ten years his senior.

"So, Tammy was when you were in high school?" Gerald asked as he scribbled on a notepad without raising his eyes.

"Right," Phillip said. "Junior and senior year."

"Virgins?" Gerald held his pencil above the paper.

"I suppose technically, yes."

Gerald looked up from his notebook.

"Yes, we were virgins," Phillip said, waving his hand forward. His mind had flashed to the nineteen-year-old waitress who had taken him back into the pantry of his parents' restaurant when he was fourteen and given him his first blowjob. It was a one-time thing that had occurred when the waitress, Crystal, was in between boyfriends. Not long afterward, she took up with a twenty-five-year-old unemployed mechanic—a "bum," Phillip's mom remarked. Phillip hung around the restaurant after school for months, pining and hoping for a repeat performance, but Crystal barely acknowledged his existence, except to offer him a bored smile now and again.

Around the holidays, his parents suspected her of using some kind of drug. "An upper," his mom said, in place of the actual term—meth, speed, coke. "She acts just like I did when I was pregnant with your brother and you. You know, the doctors put all of us on diet pills, until they finally figured out it wasn't good for us." His mother laughed, lifting her blond hair off the back of her neck and fanning the nape before letting her hair down. "It's a good thing you kids turned out so normal!"

After the new year, they suspected Crystal of fiddling with the register, which was more or less confirmed when she didn't show up for work one day. She never returned, not even to pick up her paycheck.

"It's that bum that got her hooked," his mother insisted. "She never would have done anything like that before she hooked up with that good-for-nothing. She was a good girl."

Phillip nodded, imagining what his mother would have thought if she knew what the good girl had done to her good boy in the pantry back in August. And how he would have given his entire comic book collection—a thousand comics individually wrapped in cellophane, lovingly alphabetized by title and needlessly color-coded by company (red for Marvel, blue for DC, and yellow for the independents)—for it to have happened even one more time.

Phillip was not a particularly developed fourteen-year-old.
His voice wavered across the registers, his face had only just
begun to sprout peach fuzz and acne in equal proportions, and
no matter how much he let his hair grow out like the surfer
burnouts at school, his blond hair never looked cool and be-
draggled—it just seemed to get fuller and puffier. His older
brother, Tony, whose looks more closely resembled their father's Mexican heritage than their mother's Norwegian coloring, taunted Phillip, calling him "Little Lord Fauntleroy" or
"The Little Prince." When Phillip came after him, Tony always
laughed and ducked out of the way, amused by the attempt. He
was four years older than his brother and, at that age, at least a
foot taller.

"At least no one calls me a beaner, beaner!" Phillip yelled after
Tony, who cackled as he sprinted out back into the parking lot.

"Go wash your mouth out right now." His mother had
pointed to the restaurant bathroom with a long manicured
finger. "And just be thankful your father wasn't here to hear
that."

Phillip walked to the bathroom and turned on the water,
locking the door behind him. It was doubtful his father would
have cared had he even heard him. His father had little pride
when it came to being a Mexican American. He changed the
family name from Perez to Parris—correctly assuming that the
name change would garner more respect or, at the very least,
lessen the ire reserved for Hispanics and African Americans
back then, before it was transferred to Middle Easterners. After
his *abuelita* died, the Mexican restaurant that they inherited

from Phillip's grandparents changed its menu to continental cuisine, and Parris Restaurant became known in the area as that place that served Belgian waffles all day long.

"Where did you go?" Gerald asked.

Phillip snapped his head up and then looked over at the clock Gerald kept on his desk. They had fifteen minutes left; fifteen interminable minutes with which to examine how and with such messy imprecision Phillip had ruined his life. He leaned forward and held his head in his hands.

"Do you consider Greta to be your life?" the therapist asked. His expression was neutral; nonetheless Phillip felt mocked by the question. It wasn't even his idea to see the therapist in the first place, never having put much stock in the process, but Greta would only consider marital therapy if Phillip would agree to go individually. Greta was explicit in her clarification: she would attend therapy with him but not necessarily to save their marriage. She didn't know if she even wanted to try to save it, as was evidenced by the fact that, as she told Phillip, she had been seeing another man for the past couple of months. But fifty-five minutes with her alone was worth any cost to Phillip, and he gladly paid the $260 session fee and endured Gerald's shaggy hair, sideburns, and horn-rimmed glasses.

"I've been with Greta since my first year of college. Most of my life. We met first week. Mark Twain."

"Mark Twain? The author?"

"We were the only business majors in the English elective.

Initially, I signed up for T. S. Eliot, but at the last minute I switched to Twain. I hadn't read him since grade school."

Gerald scribbled something in his notebook and then looked back at Phillip.

"That year we dressed up as Tom Sawyer and Becky Thatcher for Halloween. Her idea. We were already a couple by then." He smiled as he pictured Greta in the long blond braids and the freckles painted across the bridge of her nose with eyeliner.

"And this was at . . . ?"

"Stanford."

Gerald nodded. Phillip glanced at the certificates on the walls. UC Santa Barbara. Cal State Northridge, Class of 2000. He waited for Gerald to comment on Stanford. Most people did. The obligatory "Good school" or "Congratulations." But Gerald's face remained fixed with the same neutral expression. Except people who went to UC Santa Barbara and Cal State Northridge, apparently.

"We both went there for undergrad, and then I went directly into the GSB. Graduate School of Business," he qualified, in case Gerald wasn't familiar with the acronym. God, how proud he had always been to drop this name any chance that he got. How proud it had made his parents. How much it had tortured his brother. Gerald probably just wrote it down in his notebook, next to "self-loathing philandering husband," Phillip imagined.

"And Greta?"

"Greta applied and was accepted to every school *but* Stanford. She got into Harvard—but I didn't."

"So, she went to Harvard?"

"No. She decided to stay with me at Stanford. She ended up not going to grad school at all."

Gerald cocked his head slightly.

"Her choice, not mine." Phillip realized this sounded defensive. He remembered how much Greta's parents had resented Greta's decision not to continue her education. And she didn't even tell them about Harvard. If he were honest with himself, he could have been more supportive of Greta. Had he insisted that she go to Harvard, she probably would have gone, but both of them knew that it was unlikely that they would have stayed together. Business schools were already known as "relationship breakers" without adding three thousand miles of long distance to the equation. Greta stayed with him that first year, in the couples and family housing on the outskirts of campus, and they married at the end of August, after his consulting internship ended. During the second year, Greta commuted back and forth to Los Angeles, where she began working for a boutique advertising agency.

"Let's get back to the other women." Gerald consulted his notebook. "Marlena?"

"Marlene," Phillip corrected him.

"Marlene," Gerald repeated. He scratched the side of his face. "Tell me about her."

Phillip took a deep breath and leaned back against the itchy couch.

"Well, I cheated on Tammy to be with Marlene, and then we ended up together."

"And how long were you with Marlene?"

"Until I cheated on her to be with Greta," Phillip said. "Not long. Just the summer, really."

"A pattern . . ." Gerald said. He took off his glasses and breathed on the lenses, fogging them up and then wiping them with the corner of his shirt.

"You think?" Phillip hadn't meant for it to come out as sarcastic as it sounded. If it was detected, it went ignored.

"But then there seems to have been quite a stretch before . . ." Gerald consulted his notes. "Theresa?"

Phillip felt the muscles of his stomach involuntarily constrict. It happened every time he heard her name. How many times had he heard Greta scream Theresa's name at him or hiss it if their six-year-old daughter was in the next room. Usually, but not always, the name had an expletive or curse attached to it. "Homewrecker Theresa" or "Fucking Theresa" or "That little cunt, Theresa." Charlotte had even taken to calling her "T," correctly intuiting that somehow her beloved violin teacher's name was off-limits.

"Yes. A long time." Phillip sighed.

Gerald closed his folder and motioned toward the clock.

"We're out of time for today, Phillip, but I'd like you to think about what it is you would like to accomplish with our work together."

Phillip nodded, though he had no idea how to answer.

As if reading him, Gerald continued. "No need to answer it now, I just want you to think—"

"I want my life back," Phillip blurted out. He laughed without humor. "Can you give me that?"

Gerald arranged his face into an expression of what Phillip guessed to be encouragement. He stood up and went behind his desk, where he began shuffling papers. Phillip took this to mean that they were done and walked to the door he came in.

"Other door, Phillip." Gerald pointed to the one on the other side of the room. "Take care of yourself, and I'll see you next Tuesday."

Phillip blinked into the sunlight as he edged his Volvo out of the narrow parking garage. Feeling around for sunglasses in his pockets and then on the floor, he narrowly missed a man who had stumbled into the crosswalk pushing a cart weighed down by plastic bags overflowing with recyclables. Phillip slammed on his brakes and watched the man stumble, obliviously, to the curb. Waiting for his pulse to slow down, Phillip leaned his head against the steering wheel. A honk startled him, and he glanced back over his shoulder at the enraged driver trapped behind him. Quickly, he put the car back in gear, turned right, and drove toward Lincoln Boulevard.

At the first traffic signal, he speed-dialed his office.

"Phillip Parris." His assistant, Heather, coughed, the sound muffled as though she had stuck her thumb over the mouthpiece she wore. "Excuse me."

"I'm on my way back to the office, just getting on the freeway now."

"Oh, hang on." She put him on hold and then came right back. "I've been trying to get you. Gabe has been asking where you are."

"Shit." He put his left-hand blinker on, but the cars sped past him. "Goddammit!" He swerved into the lane anyway, and the SUV behind him slammed on its horn.

"It's okay," Heather said. "I told him you were on your way and stuck in traffic, but he's expecting you as soon as you get here."

Phillip looked at the clock on his dashboard. Two fifteen. He was at least twenty minutes away.

"What else?" he asked.

"Lee scheduled the meeting with the shared services reps for five if that's okay. I said I needed to check with you before confirming, but to go ahead and put it on the calendar."

Lee was the project leader that Phillip had assigned to the Gap account. He was one of their best and brightest, but for the first time since Phillip had been at Connelly Consulting, he had been distracted and hadn't carefully managed the project leaders. Greta had always called him a "micromanager," but as it was becoming increasingly clear to Phillip, being a micromanager simply meant doing his job.

"What about Rebecca? Was she informed we're moving her over?"

"She knows. She needs to tie up a few loose ends, and Brent is bringing her up to speed."

"Good." Phillip tapped the screen of his GPS to see what the traffic flow looked like on the way to Century City. Ropy red lines all the way to Santa Monica Boulevard. He veered off the freeway to try his luck on the side streets.

"What else?"

"Fund-raiser from Crossroads. I told her to e-mail."

"What else?"

"Um . . ." Heather hesitated.

"What?"

"Phillip, could you pull to the side of the road for a moment?"

"What is it?" The sound of Heather's voice alarmed him. "What's happened?" It was the same tone that the police officer used when they called about his parents. Phillip cut across two lanes and double-parked in front of a car wash.

"I think you were served . . . with papers. This morning, just after you left for your meeting."

Phillip felt hot and short of breath. He opened the window.

"I'm sorry," Heather said.

His throat felt dry and constricted, and he searched around the car for a water bottle. He yanked an old bottle from underneath the passenger seat and took a swig of hot, stale water, swishing it around in his mouth before spitting it out the window. Then he raised the window and pulled back into traffic, racing through a yellow light, nearly running over a nanny pushing a baby carriage, who raised a furious fist at him.

"Tell Gabe I'll be there in ten," he said, and hung up.

_____

During his rapid ascent up the ladder to managing partner at Connelly Consulting, Phillip traveled nearly every week. Chicago, Houston, Philadelphia, San Francisco, Atlanta, New York, Miami, Minneapolis, Dallas . . . Each assignment lasted anywhere from two weeks to six months, and for almost the entire duration, Phillip would fly out of LAX on Sunday night (to be there for eight a.m. meetings) and return to LAX on Friday afternoon. Every Monday morning, he would wake up and stumble to the door of the hotel to find the morning paper just so he could remind himself what city he was in. The first year alone he racked up so many frequent flier miles, he had enough to surprise Greta with a weekend getaway to Cabo San Lucas for her birthday.

The irony did not escape him that in all of those early years of incessant travel, layovers, hotel brunches and bars, Phillip had avoided the lure of an affair. His resistance had less to do with personal integrity than the fact that in those lean, magical years his desire for Greta had been stronger. The sweet moments at the end of the day when he would hear her voice from a great distance reminded him of how good their lives were, how different from their parents', making him long to be back home tangled up in her in their tiny rented house in the canyons.

One year, after spending forty-eight hours in JFK over Christmas, Phillip arrived home and climbed onto the mattress on the floor where she slept. She was naked under the covers with one slim pale leg draped over the top like a comma. He

started at her bare ankle and kissed his way up her leg until he
found the sweet and damp center of her. She stirred and murmured his name in her sleep.

"You're home . . ."

Her compliance in those days was intoxicating to him. After
what seemed to be a lifetime of Tony's hand-me-downs, at last
there was something he desired that was his and his alone.
Would it have been so exciting had she not been so full of
promise herself? The fact that Greta gave up her own career for
him made her acquiescence that much sweeter. She wasn't like
the other girls—the Jennifers and Caitlyns who went to university, majoring in communications as a ruse to meet a successful husband. Greta was driven to succeed herself. When she
inexplicably gave it up for him, he had never felt so important
in his life. He knew even then that it was probably unwise not
to encourage her to continue. Her mother actually called him
on the phone, unbeknownst to Greta, asking him to convince
Greta not to give up her studies; Phillip lied and told her that
he had tried but Greta's decision was final, and he was power-
less to dissuade her.

And so while Phillip put himself on the career fast-track,
scrambling to rise from associate to consultant to project leader
and all the way up to the holy grail of managing partner, Greta
put all of her focus on their domestic life. While Phillip made
spreadsheets at work to restructure divisions and companies,
Greta applied the same single-mindedness to building their
home and family. They agreed that they would wait to have
kids until he at least became a project leader, but Greta's deter-

mination to create the perfect life for them became all-consuming. It seemed that one day, he wasn't sure when exactly, Phillip felt like an outsider in his own marriage. The "family" loomed as a rival for her attention, a separate entity that dwarfed and overwhelmed him.

There was a brief spell just after the birth of Charlotte when the mutual enchantment of their daughter mimicked the intensity of their early years together, but this fleeting magical period was followed by years of frustration as they attempted to make a sibling for her. Charlotte's brother was supposed to be born exactly two years later, according to Greta's strict timeline, and when they missed this deadline, Greta's resolve for a larger family only intensified. As time passed, Greta became more and more preoccupied with a second child. Phillip would return home from work to find her in bed with the computer on her lap, reading fertility websites while their four-year-old daughter circled around her like a jackal, vying for her attention. He arranged lavish weekends for them to spend together as romantic distractions, but Greta seemed removed and distant. Every conversation seemed to revolve around the same cringe-inducing subjects: sperm motility and ovulatory dysfunction. One night, after he had stayed up until four thirty in the morning to complete a presentation, Greta nudged him awake to get his opinion on her cervical fluid.

"Is it copious and thinner than usual?" she asked, lying before him, legs spread.

He rubbed his eyes and tried to reconcile this view of his wife. The suggestive position completely devoid of all sexuality.

"Thinner than what exactly?" he asked. "I don't know what to compare it to."

"Go ahead, check," she insisted. She backed up onto her elbows. "They say it's supposed to be like rubber cement." He reluctantly dipped his fingers in and tried to ascertain if it was the correct consistency.

"Yeah, I guess it's rubber cement-ish," he offered. "Can I go back to sleep now?"

"After," she said, pulling him on top of her. But he wasn't ready, and her impatience only served to deflate him further.

"I'm really tired, honey," he said, shifting himself away from her. "I'm sorry."

"The chances are better in the morning," she reminded him, grasping him in her fist and handling his penis as if it were a switch connected to a lightbulb that had recently burned out. Up, down. Up, down.

He closed his eyes, resigned, and pictured the caramel-skinned waitress at the pool with the pretty gap between her two front teeth. Smiling, she had leaned over him that afternoon as she delivered his vodka tonic, her skin smelling of cocoa butter and salt, the scent lingering after she had moved on to another table. It might have been the sun or the vodka or possibly a combination of both, but in her smile Phillip had imagined a whisper of invitation.

By the time Theresa had arrived in their life, he was starving. Despite what he had told Gerald, he had already had affairs, but they were confined to a weekend here and there. He could barely remember their names or any distinguishing features. As soon as the hunger was satiated, the memory of them went into a box deep in the recesses of his mind and disappeared. Each time he swore was the last, and it conversely gave him the impetus and determination to try harder in his marriage. Each time he found that his love for Greta was enflamed just a little bit, and it made all of the little resentments he was harboring seem less important, almost trivial. He was so relieved and thankful every time he strayed to find that he had not been caught, that his marriage was still intact, that Greta's good qualities came into focus again, the snap of her sharp analytical mind mixed with her unexpected easy laugh. Suddenly, his heart gladdened to watch her doing something as simple as reading a book, stirring a sauce, or washing their daughter's hair. But soon, against his own volition, he found himself resenting her for his getting away with it. It seemed like further proof of how removed from him she was. If she didn't notice that, then what was she seeing at all? And in this state of self-delusion and justification, the little resentments piled up again, one after the other, brick after brick, until a wall of grievances stood between them, and the only way to break through it was to have another something else on the side.

Theresa had been coming to teach Charlotte for four months before Phillip said much of anything to her. He barely even registered her presence except for the occasional "Sounds good" or "Good job." She always seemed vaguely startled whenever he spoke to her, and when she answered, he often had to ask her to repeat herself. Her voice was tremulous and she blushed easily.

It was just after a year that Theresa had been teaching Charlotte that he found himself alone with her. Greta had gone to her parents' in Washington to help them with her nephew who was detoxing for the first time. Phillip arrived home and relieved the Venezuelan sitter, and then Theresa and his daughter emerged from her room laughing as Charlotte imitated a girl from school singing a song from *Mamma Mia*.

He realized that he was going to have to pay her, but he was embarrassed that he had given all his cash to the sitter.

"If you don't have to go anywhere in a hurry, I can run to the ATM," he said.

Theresa smiled and waved her hand "I don't care. Really. You can pay me next time."

He noticed that her hair was shorter than it had been the last time he had seen her. Her shiny dark hair was just under her chin rather than at her shoulders.

"Did you cut your hair?" he asked her on impulse.

She reached up and ran a hand through her hair, pulling on the ends as if she could lengthen it.

"She looks like my American Girl doll!" Charlotte squealed.

"Mistake," Theresa said. "I wasn't thinking."

"I like it," he told her.

He wasn't exactly sure why he told her this since he had vaguely preferred her hair the other way, but immediately Theresa blushed and the color spread across her cheeks and the pale skin on her chest. When he saw the flush, he realized that of course that was why he told her.

Even though he had work to complete that night after putting Charlotte to bed, he asked Theresa if she was hungry; when she solemnly nodded, he asked if she was okay with Chinese. He rarely ever ate Chinese food anymore, usually bowing to Greta's preference for Italian or French, so he was extravagant and over-ordered for the two of them. While waiting for the food to arrive, Phillip began to get Charlotte ready for bed. Since he was rarely alone with Charlotte, Theresa correctly intuited his need and offered to help. They sat on his daughter's bed, on either side of her, and read the children's encyclopedia on animals. Even then, he should have seen that the betrayal had begun. The ease with which they play-parented together was actually more disarming, in retrospect, than the sex, which didn't occur until days later. She returned on Thursday for Charlotte's next lesson, and when he invited her over the following night, after Charlotte had gone to bed, on some slim pretext (a book on Stravinsky?), there was more Chinese, more blushing. Theresa's voice became stronger, her gaze more direct. By the time they fell into each other, panting and wordless, it seemed preordained, as most affairs are wont to. She came to see him every night after that first time, except for the night when he had a group dinner with his team on the Kaiser Pharmaceutical case. If she had anything else to do at all, she canceled it. The night before Greta returned, he walked Theresa out to her car and asked when he would see her again.

"Whenever you want to," she told him.

They resorted to invented business trips and hotels after that. One night, when Theresa's sister and her boyfriend were out of town, he slept over on the fold-out couch in their Venice house. It was teenaged squalor and brought him back to the dizzying days and nights of undergrad life, when he and Greta still lived in different houses, shared with numerous roommates. Even though most of their classmates came from moneyed families, the families had all adopted a Horatio Alger work ethic when it came to their living conditions, and the students lived in a pleasant, self-imposed shabbiness.

At Theresa's sister's house, Phillip observed it all with nostalgia. The vintage rock posters, the wallpaper curled in the corners, the air-conditioner leaking fluid in a dark trickle along the wall. An Obama Chia pet with a dead afro languishing on a windowsill.

"Pass me the bong?" Phillip joked.

Theresa was flustered and on the verge of tears. She seemed so self-conscious and uncomfortable that he booked a room the following night at Shutters on the Beach, an upscale resort hotel nearby. They spent the weekend shut up in the room together, ordering in room service and watching pay-per-view films. He had told Greta that he was in Detroit.

Looking back, those two days were essentially the apogee of his relationship, affair, transgression—whatever one wanted to call what he had with Theresa. After that, she took possession of him like a virus that he couldn't shake. She became increasingly demanding about when she would see him next. Where would the next hotel rendezvous be? How long could he spend with her? Could she tell her sister about him? If she felt him retreating from her, she became sullen and punitive. At the end of every interaction they had, Phillip was left with the queasy, uneasy sense that she was a firearm waiting to go off. At any moment, she might lose control and tell Greta the truth. He hastened to placate Theresa, taking ridiculous risks—leaving work in the middle of the day, sneaking out of bed in the middle of the night, doing everything to buy himself one more day of keeping his marriage intact.

In the first weeks of their affair, Phillip had provided her with a work e-mail address that Greta never had the access nor the inclination to check, but on that one horrible day Theresa accidentally—or perhaps purposefully—chose to write Phillip an e-mail and send it to his home Gmail account. This was the account reserved for scheduling family outings, Charlotte's doctor's appointments, fertility meetings, anniversaries, car repairs, and swimming lessons. It was to this address that Theresa wrote the words "i don't get what i am to you" in twenty lowercase letters. Had Theresa not pushed Send after the two bottles of wine that she drank before writing this, or had Greta not happened to have woken up in the morning to her own frozen MacBook and needed to sign out of Phillip's e-mail account before accessing hers; had he ended it when he should have or, better yet, never even started it—Phillip's mind reeled imagining how different his life would be now had the series of events failed to occur in just the order that they had. But they hadn't, and the convergence of these eight simple words with Greta's chance discovery brought down the life they built together as swiftly as a structure made of Tinkertoys kicked over by an impetuous two-year-old child.

Marital therapy was briskly arranged, and in the days leading up to the appointment, Phillip attempted to invent lies upon lies, fearing that if he admitted to even *one* indiscretion, it would all be over.

"Why would she write such a thing to you?" Greta demanded. "Is she crazy? Has something happened between you? Are you in love with her?"

It was this last question that he was able to answer honestly. No, he didn't love her. Of course he didn't. He clung to this small shred of sincerity while he tried to hold Greta close to him, grasping for her with the desperation of a condemned man who knows that he has little chance for a stay of execution.

But by the time they arrived at the therapist's office, in that moment when Phillip sank into the oversized club chair, he was so tired of his fear of being caught, so tired from the nights without sleep and the exhaustion of living multiple lives, he felt in that moment that to lose Greta would be preferable to continuing the grueling, fearful deception that had gradually and brutally overtaken his life.

"I don't know what to say," he said, covering his face with his hands.

Greta sat across from him, rigid. Her jaw was set and she looked as though she were ready to spring at him with some supernatural power, as though she were a comic book character from the volumes he had devoured as a teen. But she remained silent, attempting to hold in her emotions, Phillip supposed, out of deference to the therapist, a kindly-looking older woman with short gray hair.

"Just tell the truth, Phillip," the woman said in a voice that sounded slightly Southern in origin.

"Oh God, Oh God, Oh God . . ." he moaned, rocking back and forth.

He looked up at the fear and sadness in Greta's face. The rigidity in her jaw started to fail and she began to tremble.

"Go on," the therapist urged like a mantra. "Tell the truth, Phillip."

He glanced anxiously at the Buddha statues and orchids strewn about the office. There was a crushing silence in the room, briefly interrupted by the percussive sound of a truck backing up in the alleyway. Then more silence.

"I'm so sorry, Greta," he finally said.

"So it's true?" she whispered. "You and Theresa?"

He nodded faintly, and wiped the wetness off his face with the back of his sleeve. He wasn't sure if he was crying or perspiring or both. The therapist stood and handed him a tissue box.

"What's true, exactly?" Greta said. Her voice sounded very small, as though issuing from a great distance. "Was it just—"

"All of it. Everything. I'm sorry."

Greta nodded. The color had drained from her face. Her eyes were glassy and out of focus, her mouth slightly open. She looked like someone whose house was burning down in front of her, deciding what possessions to take with her.

"Stay here with me, both of you. Just breathe for a moment," the therapist said, and took deep, illustrative breaths, urging the two of them to do the same.

Phillip watched Greta clutching at her stomach. He got down on his knees in front of her.

"I'm so sorry. Greta, believe me when I tell you, I'm so sorry. I'll never do anything like this again." He took her right hand in his. She stared at his hand and fingered his wedding ring, turning it around with her own index finger.

"Did you keep this on when you did it?"

He looked at the therapist, confused, unsure of what to say, how to answer. The therapist nodded her head to continue.

"I've never taken this off," he said to Greta. "Not in eighteen years. Never."

Greta nodded, her lip curling upward—it was the faintest snarl of contempt, the first of its kind he had ever seen from her.

"Please go away. Please just get away from me," she groaned.

"Greta . . ."

"Now!" Her voice came out like a strangled roar.

"Hold on, Greta," the therapist said. "It's okay. You're okay. Stay with us."

Phillip quickly moved back to his chair and looked to the therapist for direction. She folded her hands in her lap and nudged her Plexiglas chair a little closer to them.

"What else does Greta need to know?" she said. "Were there others?"

Phillip hesitated. Greta stared at him, unblinking.

"The truth comes out eventually," the therapist said. "It always does."

She let the weight of this hang in the air for a moment before continuing.

"And if there is ever a chance of repairing what has been broken between you two, your wife needs to have the truth in its entirety."

"I don't think that's possible," he said.

"The truth?" she said, "Or repairing what is broken."

"Both," he said.

"You both deserve the truth," the woman said. "Both of you." She turned to Greta, who faintly shrugged her shoulders in the affirmative.

And so Phillip began to confess the extent of his betrayal. The women in conferences, the interns, the one-night stands. Once he began, he found that he couldn't stop. He confessed to crimes he had committed before he had ever even known Greta. Crystal in the back pantry. Leaving Tammy's house and going straight to Marlene's while Tammy called his home repeatedly in tears. The pass he made at Marlene's older sister, Michelle, when Marlene was setting up the Dungeons & Dragons game in their basement. Each confession made him more delirious. He started confessing things that he wasn't even sure happened. The caramel gap-toothed waitress, the redheaded mother at Charlotte's school. Had something happened with her? Or had he merely noticed her with the intention of flirting later? It all became a toxic muddle of fact and fiction, and he was no more able to stop confessing than a bulimic teenager could withstand the call of purification following a slumber party. With each and every mea culpa, he caught sight of his wife recoiling, drifting further and further away from him, until he almost imagined that he could see the essence of her floating away. By the time he had finished, breathless and heaving, he was left with the distinct impression that although she hadn't moved from the seat directly facing him, she was gone. She had slipped away, like the last sliver of sun below the horizon before the sky darkens.

He had lost her.

Every route that Phillip chose to take leading back to his office was snarled with traffic. He veered off the freeway, thinking somehow it might be better, but gridlock soon greeted him there, too. Only three o'clock in the afternoon and the cars were bumping up against each other with the impatience and burgeoning panic that Los Angeles rush hour inspired. Where was everyone going? Phillip looked over at the cars idling beside him. In a blue Jetta, a woman put on makeup in her rearview mirror while talking to herself. Behind her, a heavyset man blew a gust of smoke out of his beat-up Ford Explorer, before his tattooed arm extended out the window and he flicked away a cigarette. On the other side of Phillip, a teenage girl inched forward in her Honda Accord while texting. He watched her heavily lipsticked mouth form the words *Are you fucking kidding me?* Absorbed in her reply, she failed to drive forward until the cacophony of honks startled her, and glancing up, she aggressively accelerated, rear-ending the green Mercedes less than a car length in front of her. Phillip pounded on his steering wheel and U-turned out of the lane before the imminent pileup the accident would surely cause.

He managed to get back onto the freeway in good time and was relieved to find that the traffic was much milder on this section. As he weaved his way in and out of the cars, a text from Heather arrived on his phone: ARE YOU CLOSE? He looked up at the signs spanning the five lanes of traffic to tell her his location. That was when he realized that he was on the 405 going north instead of south. He looked over at the standstill of traffic in the other direction, switched off his phone, and just kept driving.

The Parris family restaurant was located in the San Fernando Valley, nestled between a Payless shoe store and a hardware store in foreclosure. After Phillip's parents died unexpectedly in the same month ten years earlier, Phillip's brother, Tony, and his wife, Suzanne, made the decision to take over the restaurant rather than see it close. It had been in the family for three generations, and though Phillip had refused to believe he had any sentimental attachment to the place, now as he sped north away from his office and all of his adult responsibilities, he realized that he was driving toward it—the restaurant, his brother, and all that remained of his boyhood.

He parked on the street and put a couple of quarters in the meter. The restaurant was empty after the lunch rush, if there was even a lunch rush these days. A bearded man drank a glass of water in the corner, absorbed in a newspaper. Probably a homeless man, Phillip figured, but his parents had had a rule about them when he was younger.

"As long as they are polite, don't smell too much of drink, and aren't taking tables from paying customers, they are welcome here."

If they looked to be starving, Phillip's father would feed them, but only after the paying customers left and on the condition that they agreed to perform a menial task—washing dishes, taking out the trash. Usually they did; if they didn't, they were turned away.

"Everybody needs to work for something" his father insisted. "If you only take charity, it makes you die inside." It was a phrase often repeated to his two sons when they were young. Phillip remembered admiring it when he was little and then, as a teenager, rolling his eyes and dismissing it as nothing more than one of the many prosaic platitudes beloved by his father. By the time Phillip reached adulthood—which, according to Greta, had happened only recently if at all—Phillip was back to respecting his father more than any other man he had known. Phillip had struggled to find a way to tell his father this, but after working his entire life, and just before retirement, his father suffered a stroke while driving their mother home from the eye doctor. The car careened into a tree on the side of the street that held the wooden swing he and his brother had played on as children. His father died instantly. His mother spent three and a half weeks in the ICU before her heart gave out.

In the other corner of the restaurant, a young man sat writing in an open spiral notebook, with a stack of schoolbooks in front of him. It took Phillip a moment to register that this boy was his nephew, whom he hadn't seen in years.

"Anthony?"

The boy looked up from his studies. There was a similar delay as he seemed to struggle to place Phillip's face. Then, abruptly, he grinned and stood up.

"Uncle Phillip," he said, shaking his hand with a surprisingly strong grip.

"Look at you!" Phillip pulled him into an embrace and then let go as he felt the muscles in his nephew contract. Phillip remembered how awkward he felt at Anthony's age, being hugged by relatives.

"You look good, Anthony. What are you, seventeen now?"

"Sixteen. Seventeen in July."

"Right, the fifth? Same as your grandma's, isn't it?"

Anthony nodded, smiling. He went to sit down, then seemed to remember his manners, and stood back up, leaning against the table.

"Dad's in back. You want me to go get him?"

"No, I'll go. Stay and finish your homework, or whatever it is you're doing."

"Okay. Good to see you."

Phillip squeezed the boy's shoulder, then walked toward the back of the restaurant in search of his brother. A teenage girl in a white T-shirt and black skirt stopped him on the way into the kitchen.

"Can I help you, sir?" She had an eyebrow piercing, and when she spoke, Phillip could see the stud on her tongue.

Anthony called out from the corner table, "He's my uncle, Dawn. He's going to talk to Dad."

Dawn stepped aside and waved to the back. "Oh, sorry," she said. She took the pencil from behind her ear and twisted it back into her hair. Glancing over at the man nursing his water, she walked over to Anthony's table and sat down across from him.

The bones of the restaurant were the same, but some steps had been taken to upgrade a little. The earth-tone paisley wallpaper his mother had picked out had been replaced by a more contemporary abstract design, and the wood floors were stripped a shade or two lighter. Admiring the changes, Phillip walked behind the counter and through the kitchen, where a Hispanic man and woman in hairnets were prepping vegetables and washing dishes. They glanced up at Phillip, nonplussed, and went back to what they were doing.

"Is Tony back here?" he asked.

The young man gestured toward the pantry.

A moment later, Phillip's brother emerged from the pantry carrying a large sack of flour over his shoulder. His dark hair had gone completely salt-and-pepper, like their father's, and it took Phillip a moment to contain the riot of emotion he felt looking at this unexpected combination of father and brother. "Tony." He exhaled, almost inaudibly, and his brother glanced up at Phillip. The lines in his face deepened as a broad smile creased his face. The smile erupted into a wheezy ex-smoker's laugh, which he broke off abruptly when he caught sight of the anguish of his brother's expression. He dropped the flour and took hold of his brother in his arms.

Phillip felt his throat tighten and constrict.

"Felipe," he heard his brother say, pronouncing the name the way their *abuelita* did and, later, his father on the rare occasion that he drank.

Phillip collapsed into his brother, his only living immediate family, whom he hadn't seen in more than three years. The kitchen help scattered in different directions as the strangled sobs echoed throughout the stainless-steel kitchen. At the moment, it didn't matter to Phillip that he hadn't cried in front of his brother, or any other man, since he was seven years old. He just allowed himself the release and comfort of his brother's embrace, repeating the words, "I'm sorry, I'm sorry," without knowing for certain for what or to whom he was apologizing.

"I can open up one of our bottles of wine, if you'd want that instead," Tony said.

He set two cups of coffee on the side table in the kitchen. It was at this small table that the staff, Javier and Isa, ate their meal, before prepping for the next day's breakfast and lunch—

the restaurant served a local working crowd, opening at six a.m
and closing at four p.m. Today, however, Tony sent them home
early, telling them that he would finish their prep for them.
They nodded, obedient and solemn, but they looked at Phillip
with an obvious question in their eyes: Who was this strange
man in relation to their boss? Phillip watched them go, remembering all the employees his parents had hired and the few that
had been fired. The single mothers, part-time students, illegal
immigrants (always with papers, however illegitimate). They
had been a part of the family, and when they left, it was like
foster children going on to a real home. It was odd now to not
know anything about the restaurant and the members of its
strong temporary families.

"I mean, I gotta stick with the coffee," Tony continued, "and
I couldn't tell you whether it's good wine or not . . ."

Tony and his wife had met in Alcoholics Anonymous. They
had both tried and failed several times at sobriety, and on what
would have been Tony's eighth—and what he swore was his
last—serious try, they had met each other. Even though it was
advised in the first year not to have any romantic entangle-
ments, he and Suzanne fell for each other, clinging together
with an enduring gratitude for what seemed like their last
chance at survival in both life and love.

Phillip held up the coffee mug, blowing to cool it. "No, it's
okay. I'm good with this.

Tony remained standing, gesturing to the wine. "You sure?
You know it's okay with me, right? I mean, sometimes people

feel awkward. But I actually kind of like it, the smell. Red wine." He inhaled, smiling.

Phillip shook his head. "No thanks. I really don't want any. I don't know *why*, with all this . . ."

He took a sip of coffee without finishing his sentence, searching for the right word to properly describe what had become of his life.

"Calamity," he said at last.

Tony came and sat across from him.

"What did she do?" he asked, and then smacked his forehead. "Oh, jeez. Suzanne would bust me for being sexist right now. Is that sexist?" Out of the corner of his eye, he noticed the napkin holder on the table askew. Zeroing in on it, he righted the napkin holder, then straightened the napkins that had been sticking out. He looked back at Phillip. "I think about that now, with Sarah. So she respects herself, you know. Fifteen is a hell of a time, let me tell you. Just *wait*." He shook his head and mock shuddered.

"I don't know about sexist," Phillip said. "But as it happens, it wasn't her. It was me."

His brother nodded, the corners of his mouth turned down, but Phillip didn't feel that his brother was frowning at him. It was just what happened to his face with age. Calamities pulled the corners of the mouth down. His own face probably did it, but he never had the occasion or the desire to really look at himself.

"Got it," Tony said. "You can tell me all the details. Or none of them. Okay? I'm here."

Phillip nodded.

Tony reached across the table and ran his knuckles across Phillip's jawline. Another gesture of his father's. When did his brother become their father? And if Phillip wasn't even remotely his father, then who was he?

"I mean it," Tony said.

"Okay." Phillip took a drink of coffee. "Thanks."

"How's Greta? Are you two still . . ."

"She served me with papers. Today."

"Today?" Tony raised his eyebrows. "*Today*, today?"

"Is there another one?" Phillip said. "Yeah. About three hours ago. Maybe more. I wasn't there. It was at my office."

"Jesus." Tony shook his head. "I'm sorry." He was quiet for a moment, running his thumb back and forth over his chapped lower lip. "Is there anything you can do? Or is it—let me put it this way . . . do you want out of this, too?"

Phillip thought for a moment. It seemed crazy to say it, considering everything he had done, every time he had pretended in his mind not to be married, but now he wanted his marriage more than he had ever wanted anything. More than his job, which he was perilously close to losing if he continued this erratic behavior; more than the freedom he had once imagined he had lost; more than he had wanted to marry Greta in the first place, which at the time had seemed monumental. The only thing equal to the enormity of his want was his regret.

"I know—" Phillip's voice broke. He coughed into his sleeve. "I know that everything can't go back to the way it was— obviously, there was something . . . wrong. Or not right." He paused and considered the distinction. "But I love her. Desperately. And I think we could get over this. That's the thing. I know I can get over it. I'm a different person now. . . ."

Tony was silent. Phillip ran his hands through his hair and dropped them to the table.

"It's just, she can't get over it. Not yet, at least. If ever . . . I don't know."

"Does she know how much you want the marriage?" Tony asked.

"Of course. I've told her a hundred times. A thousand. Doesn't seem to matter." Phillip shook his head. "I don't blame her. And probably the kindest thing that I could do at this point would be just to get the hell out of her life." He rubbed his eyes, and then closed them, pressing his two thumbs against the sockets. "But as it's become abundantly clear to just about anyone I have come into contact with, I'm not a kind person."

If Tony took this to be self-pity, or an invitation to contradict his brother, he gave no indication.

"Does Charlotte know?"

"No. But she's used to the separation. I got an apartment back in September."

"Wow." Tony looked up at the right-hand corner of the ceiling, doing the mental math.

"Five months," Phillip said.

Tony sighed. He reached across the small table and squeezed Phillip's shoulder.

"I'm sorry. You and Greta. God, I don't even remember when you *weren't* together.

"And you were wasted for a lot of it," Phillip said, with a weary grin. He remembered the mod tuxedo that Tony had worn to their wedding, instead of the one rented expressly for him. He had stumbled into the wedding processional and given a toast at dinner so rambling and inappropriate that Greta's mother had made Greta's father unplug the amp.

Tony laughed. "Yeah, well . . ."

Phillip smiled at his brother. Even though both he and Greta had been furious at him for a few months after the wedding, it had made for consistently funny anecdotes at dinner parties.

"How's Suzanne?" Phillip asked.

"She's good, thanks. You just missed her, actually. She went to take Sarah somewhere. Some doctor. They were secretive about it, so I didn't ask."

Phillip tried to imagine Charlotte growing breasts, getting her period, driving a car to meet a boyfriend. His own daughter turning into a woman was as impossible for him to imagine as animals standing up on their hind legs and speaking.

"She cares a lot about Sarah and her self-esteem," Tony said. "Reading all these books and underlining them for me. She wants her to respect herself—not do all this crazy shit these kids are doing now with the *sexting*."

"She's not doing that, is she?"

Phillip flashed back to the picture that Theresa has sent him, posing topless with her honey-colored violin in her lap. He shuddered now, recalling how stirred he had been by the image before erasing it from his phone and asking her not to do it again. It wasn't because he didn't desire it, but having that picture on the little square window of his phone made the affair more real somehow. Looking at the photo made it harder for Phillip to convince himself that the affair was insignificant and safely confined, that it existed only in the dark, hidden places of his life.

"Naw. She knows better than that," Tony said. He sighed and finished his coffee, but in that sigh Phillip heard all of the fear and heartbreak of a father who knows he is losing his daughter. Worse, he recognized that sorrowful certainty that no matter how parents may strive to protect their children, they will be hurt, somehow, in some way—most likely from their own doing. It made him think of how Greta, strung-out and hormonal, had watched over baby Charlotte sleeping and burst into tears at the thought that one day pain would find her and there was nothing they would be able to do to stop it.

"It's a sort of terrorism," Greta sobbed, wild-eyed and irrational.

Phillip had held her then, telling her that together they would protect Charlotte. She would be fine—more than fine, she would flourish. Utilizing all of the simple and reasonable reassurances he could access at the time, he had managed to allay her fear, never imagining that he would be the one who would succeed in harming their daughter, when his failings tore apart their family.

Greta, for her part, was more than willing to inform Phillip of his culpability when it came to the damage done to their daughter. Though the shock of betrayal had initially silenced Greta, when her voice did return, it was almost unrecognizable to Phillip. In eighteen years of marriage, he could count on

one hand the number of times that either of them had raised
their voice at the other. But for weeks on end he found himself
frightened and cowed by the hysterical, keening woman who
had taken possession of his wife. And then, when he had resigned himself to this person into whom Greta had transformed, he was struck by yet another metamorphosis. An eerie
calm descended over her, as cold and disheartening as the early
morning fog that strips the warmth from the Los Angeles sky.

"You are the kind of man we want to protect our daughter
from," she had said.

Tony took their empty mugs and rinsed them out in the sink.
Then he headed over to the counter and began the next day's
prep. He lifted up a soft, wet box of bell peppers and placed it
within reach. Calmly, with the easy confidence of a man who
has completed this task ten thousand times, he took a curved
serrated blade and cored out a green pepper. He gave it a little
shake, dislodging the flimsy white seeds, and placed the pepper
upside down on the counter. Phillip watched his brother move
through the contents of the box with a steadiness that could
have been hunger or artistry or just mindless persistence; whatever it was, it soothed Phillip. He was reminded of the hours
spent in his parents' restaurant as a child, racing around under-
foot while the formidable figures of his mother and father
peeled, sliced, assembled, boiled, sauteed, baked, and broiled
an array of dishes as eternally familiar to him as the smell of his
mother's lilac perfume.

Tony was halfway through the box when Phillip got up to join him. It had been a long time since he had raised a hand in a kitchen, and he was surprised how quickly it came back, how natural the paring knife felt in his right hand, the back of the blade pressing against the bottom of his index finger, the slight juice of the vegetable dribbling onto the counter. He wiped his forehead with his sleeve and smiled at his brother, little and paternal beside him, and he continued slicing. One by one he placed the hollowed-out peppers in a cluster. Some of them had been poorly sliced and tipped over, spilling their imperfect emptiness onto the counter. He left those where they fell.

THE PLACES YOU DON'T WALK AWAY FROM

From: GretaParris@gmail.com
Subject: Fwd:
Date: August 1 2011 3:45:41 AM PDT
To: PhillipParris@gmail.com

PARRIS GRETA
PARRIS PHILLIP
543 Amalfi Drive
Los Angeles, CA 90402

Dear Clients,

Our records indicate that you have 6 frozen embryo(s)
in storage at our facility at West Coast Fertility Center–
Los Angeles since 9/1/2010.

If you wish to continue to store your embryos at our facility,
simply pay the invoice and sign and return this letter by
12/1/2011.

If you choose any other option, please return the letter with
your notarized signatures.

- Keep all of our frozen embryos in storage until
  further notice. (Please enclose storage fees.)

- Thaw and discard all of our frozen embryos.
- Make all of our frozen embryos available for Anonymous Embryo Donation.
- Donate embryos for Stem-Cell Research.

Please print your name and sign in the appropriate spaces.

Partner # 1: GRETA PARRIS

Signature: _____ Date: _____

Partner # 2: PHILLIP PARRIS

Signature: _____ Date: _____

Notary Public Seal:

_____

(Please state if you are notarizing one patient's signature or both.)

Medical Director: M. Dunne, MD
3521 Olympic Blvd. Suite 400 Los Angeles, CA 90402
Tel 310.555.3212 Fax: 310.555.3211
www.wcfcla.com

Greta lay on her side curled up like a shell. It had been almost a year since she had shared the bed with anyone. In the beginning, when Phillip had first moved out, she had told herself to relish the great expanse of the bed; but it was a hollow prompt, and she would wake in the middle of the night to find herself flush along the right edge. It was a habit of confinement that she could not and—later, even after meeting Peter—would not break. Whenever Charlotte stayed at her father's and Greta invited Peter over for the night, she insisted that they sleep in the guest room. She knew that Peter saw it as a residual sentimentality, and Greta didn't bother to argue the point. Peter was probably right. She didn't know why she should be sentimental toward the bed, when it was the same bed her husband had lain in with Theresa—a fact that she found herself almost able to block from her mind, except when she was about to do the same thing with another man. Men are different about these things, Peter had told her. They don't think about the appropriateness of where they are about to cheat.

"It stands to reason that if he took the time to consider how wrong it was to fuck her in his marital bed, he probably wouldn't have done it at all," Peter said.

Greta nodded but said nothing. She didn't like talking about Phillip with Peter, or about Peter with Phillip.

As much as Greta longed for another hour of sleep, the early morning light shone through the wooden blinds and striated across the floor in jagged stripes. The cat, Thinmuffin (christened by a three-year-old Charlotte), as if sensing Greta's wakefulness began mewling at the door of the terrace, and Charlotte herself would be up within the hour. Greta dragged herself out of bed and went to the terrace door to let the cat in. The gray cat stood at the door, tail twitching, and deposited a bluebird at her feet on her way into the room. Greta knelt down and examined the bird. The wing, dampened by blood, jutted out at a sharp angle and she noticed one of the eyes was scratched out. The heart, she was sorry to find, was still beating.

After dropping off Charlotte at summer camp, Greta returned home to find a large moving van in front of the house next door. A crew of men was carrying chairs and side tables out to the open doors of the truck and wheeling them up the ramp on a dolly. She slowed down her car and peered into the yard to see if she could see her neighbor, the old lady whom Charlotte had befriended. She wondered if she was moving into a home. Greta knew very little about her other than the few random things that she had gleaned from Charlotte.

A woman in a white button-down shirt and jeans came out of the house and chatted with a man who looked to be the head mover. The woman turned to follow him inside and then noticed Greta idling in the car. Greta unrolled the window as the woman approached.

"Hi, are you the little girl's mother?"

"Yes. Charlotte," Greta said.

"Nice to meet you, Charlotte," she said, "I'm Amanda."

"No, no. Sorry, I'm Greta. Charlotte's my daughter."

Amanda tapped her forehead with the heel of her open palm. "Yes, I knew that. I'm sorry, I'm a little scattered."

"Is everything okay?" Greta glanced over at a burly muscled man carrying what looked like a headboard. "Is your mother moving? It's your mother who lives here, isn't it?" Greta stopped as she searched for her name. "I've never really spoken to her, though my daughter has been over quite a bit."

"My mother died. A week ago." Amanda turned and yelled over to a pregnant woman who had just emerged from the house. "Don't let them move the piano till I'm in there!"

"Oh God," Greta said. "I'm so sorry." She felt that she had just seen the old woman pruning her garden in her funny hat.

The pregnant woman carefully navigated down the porch steps, holding on to the wooden railing for support. "Not to worry, *tesoro*," she called out with an Italian accent. As she waddled her way over to Amanda, she squinted to see into the car. Amanda put her hand on the woman's stomach. Then she picked it up and moved it to another spot, as if trying to feel the baby's movement. Greta remembered Phillip's hands on her belly when she was carrying Charlotte and experienced such a searing sadness and envy that she could feel her eyes burn as they involuntarily filled with tears.

"Thank you," Amanda said. "Greta, this is my partner, Francesca."

Francesca extended her hand to Greta.

"Hello," she said.

"Greta is our neighbor," Amanda said. "Her little girl is the one Mom was always going on about."

"So you're moving in?" Greta asked.

"For now," Amanda said. "At least until we are ready to sell. If the market ever turns around."

Greta felt a small surge of disappointment. It was a feeling

that she remembered, acutely, from when she was a girl nego-
tiating the tricky waters of girlhood friendship. At one time
female friendship had been paramount to her. She and her
friend April had been nearly inseparable until they had moved
away to college, and it was only recently that Greta noticed the
marked absence of friends in her life—female or otherwise.
Her marriage had sufficiently obscured this deficit. Now she
craved the intimacy of friends but felt ill equipped to make
them. It seemed that her six-year-old daughter was infinitely
more skilled than Greta.

"I would love to stay in this neighborhood," Francesca offered. "It seems perfect for the children." She looked at Amanda,
whose expression remained neutral, and then smiled at Greta.
"But you know . . . it's more complicated for Amanda."

One of the movers came up and stood hovering behind the
women.

"Sorry to interrupt," he said. "When you have a minute?"

Amanda raised her hand to the man. "Be right there," she
said. "Nice to meet you, Greta." She followed the man back
into the house.

Francesca stayed behind. She reached out her thumb and
rubbed it across a bright blue smear of paint that had been left
by another car.

"Perhaps after we settle a bit, we might have you over for an
aperitivo, a drink?" Francesca arched her back with one palm
held flat against her sacrum and the other hand spread across
her belly like a fan.

"I'd love that," Greta said.

She drove up the hill to the big empty house. At the top of the driveway, Thinmuffin lay on her back, licking her paws and staring up at the hummingbirds feeding in the overgrown bottlebrush tree. Since they had adopted the cat three years ago, she had managed to kill an astonishing array of birds. Crows, warblers, sparrows, and scrub jays had all fallen prey to the executioner that was their twelve-pound, slightly over-weight tabby.

As Greta let herself into the house, she turned and looked at the cat lolling in the sun, watching the hummingbirds hover in the trees above the cat's half-closed eyes and swishing tail. It was the only avian species that the cat had failed to kill, and it made Greta wonder if animals were capable of understanding futility. Or perhaps, unlike us, they just inherently better understand the importance of timing.

"I'm just disappointed, is all."

Peter picked the radishes out of his salad and piled them up on the side of his plate. "I thought we were driving up the coast after you dropped Charlotte off."

Greta swirled the straw around in her iced tea and looked out over the boardwalk to the water. "I'm sorry. I should have told you before. It's just that—"

"It's okay," he interrupted. "I have stuff to do in the apartment anyway. This apartment isn't going to furnish itself."

"Let me finish," Greta said.

After years of altering the way she spoke with Phillip, she

found it aggravating now whenever it felt that she was not fully expressing herself. She didn't like to be interrupted, analyzed, or manipulated—none of which Peter was doing, she hastened to remind herself. She looked back at him and smiled. "I am sorry. I've been putting this off, and we really need to talk."

Peter nodded. "Sure, sure. Of course." He looked down and pushed the lettuce around and then absently took a bit of radish and chewed on it. Greta wondered why he had pushed all of the radishes onto the corner of his plate. She had assumed that the segregation of food had to do with dislike, the way that Charlotte separated her food, leaving all of the greenery for last in the hopes that Greta wouldn't notice the offending vegetables.

"I just forget sometimes," he said.

"Why do you do that?" Greta asked.

Peter looked startled. "What?"

"Smush all of the radishes to the side like that. Do you like them or not?"

"As it happens, I've always harbored an intense dislike for them."

She waited for more. "And?"

"I still do," he said.

Greta laughed. His face relaxed at the triumph of having elicited the response. His delight in delighting her was a trait that she found alternately charming and galling. It felt at times like she was an audience of one and that a sign was being held up instructing her to applaud.

"I think it's important to continue to investigate how you feel, what you think," Peter said. "It changes all the time."

She rolled her eyes. "O wise one."

"I am wise, little grasshopper," he said. He motioned to the waiter for a refill of water.

"What do you always forget?" she asked him.

"What?"

"You said that you always forget something."

Peter shook his head. "Oh, yeah . . . whatever."

"Not whatever. What?"

"That you're married."

He seemed to be waiting for some kind of reassurance. She knew that he wanted her to tell him that it was not for long, that she didn't love Phillip. Instead, she said, "It shouldn't be an all-day thing. We're going to have coffee while Charlotte is in art class, and then take her to the airport at five. He can take her, but it's the first time she's flying by herself and . . ."

"You want to be there," Peter supplied.

"Yes." She turned her face to the sun and felt the heat burning along her eyelids, creating strange patterns in her vision. "It's hard to explain."

"You don't have to," he said. He held out a crust of bread to a mangy-looking pigeon that had landed on the railing. It pecked the crust out of his hands. Immediately a swarm of other pigeons descended upon the bird and the bread, fighting for their share.

At the appointed hour, Phillip waited for Greta in the coffee-house across from Charlotte's art class. He tried to focus on the case in front of him, mulling over data that required multiple rereads before he could extract any of its meaning. Discrepancies in the two columns had just begun to appear when Charlotte flew into his arms. He inhaled chlorine and sunscreen as her long, wet hair whipped across his face.

"Daddy!" Her cry was muffled into his neck.

"There's my girl," he said. He looked up at Greta, who stood a few paces behind Charlotte. "Hi," he said.

Greta blinked and said nothing. She pulled up the jeans that were falling down off her hips. It was the thinnest that Phillip had seen her since they had been in college together, but her face had a healthy color. Sprinkled across the bridge of her nose was the band of freckles that always came out when she spent time at the beach. He had overheard Charlotte telling one of her school friends that her mother's friend had just gotten an apartment on the water, but he had restrained himself from seeking more information.

"I know we're a few minutes late," she said, "but there was a highly competitive game of Marco Polo going on. . . ."

Phillip stood up, lifting Charlotte up in his arms. She was too old to be carried this way, but Phillip enjoyed it too much to stop. Charlotte flailed excitedly, her elbow knocking into a man who was carrying a tray of drinks.

"Whoa!" The man steadied his tray.

Phillip lowered Charlotte back to the ground. She scrambled into her father's seat and placed his sunglasses on her face.

"Charlotte, what do you say?" Greta prompted.

"Sor-ry," Charlotte told the man.

"Why don't I just run her over there and I'll meet you right back here, okay?" Phillip said, reaching out his hand for the sunglasses. With a precise pout, Charlotte deposited them onto his palm.

Greta draped her jacket on the back of a chair. She sat down and began scrolling through her phone.

"Would you order for me?" Phillip asked.

"I don't know what you want," she said, without looking up at him.

"The usual."

She looked up at him and he saw her eyes flash. "I don't know what the usual is," she said.

"I'll order when I get back," he said quickly. "Come on, honey," he said, taking Charlotte's hand.

Phillip and Charlotte walked across the street to the children's art studio. He turned and looked at Greta watching them through the window, but her expression was obscured by the sunlight reflecting in the glass.

When he returned, he sat down across from her. She had ordered him a double espresso, and she held a mug of something hot in her hands.

"Thanks," he said.

"How did she go to class?"

"Fine, fine. There were only two other kids there."

Greta took a sip of tea. "She hasn't been so good lately. I don't know if you've noticed or not." She looked at him, and he braced himself for the accusation. "I think she's depressed."

Phillip took a deep breath. He exhaled slowly, taking a moment to compose what he would say. Most conversations with Greta outside a therapist's office deteriorated in a matter of minutes. It didn't even have to be about something as important as their daughter. It could be a trivial comment: "I went to the market and they were out of eggs." This would be followed up by Greta demanding, "Did you ever go shopping with her? Did she cook for you?"

"Charlie doesn't seem . . . depressed," he began. "She seems a little angry. Aggressive."

"Depression is expressed as anger in children," Greta said. "It's what her pediatrician said anyway when I took her in for her checkup."

Phillip removed a sugar packet from the wooden container on the side of the table and poured the contents into the espresso. He stirred it with a wooden stick. "Do you think we should bring her in to talk to someone?"

Greta sighed. "I don't know. Maybe. I don't think she'll go by herself, so we would need to go with her."

"I figured we would."

She looked out the window. A woman with five dogs on two leashes navigated her way through families pushing wide colorful strollers down the busy sidewalk. Greta sighed and shook her head.

"This is not how I saw us turning out," she said. "Our family. You and me."

"It's not too late," Phillip said. "Please, Greta." He reached across the table and took her hand in his. To his surprise, she allowed her hand to be held for a moment before removing it.

"Your lawyer told mine that once we get through the discovery process . . ." she began. Her eyes filled with tears. He reached for her again, but this time she pushed his hand away. "We need to decide what to do with the . . ." She modulated her voice lower as her eyes darted to the other tables. "Embryos," she finished quickly.

"I know," Phillip said.

"Did you get that form I sent you?"

"I did," Phillip took a sip of coffee. It tasted even more bitter than usual. He took another packet and tore it open. He half waited for Greta to remind him of the threat of diabetes that ran in his family. She watched him pour the packet into his coffee, silent.

"Do we have to decide this now?" he asked.

"It needs to be in our divorce agreement."

"Oh God, Greta. I don't want this." He put his head in his hands.

"What do you want, Phillip?"

"I want you. I want our family. I want . . ."

She glared at him. "At what point exactly, Phillip, did you decide to want me? Was it when you took her to bed the first time? The second time? Is it—" She stopped herself and looked down at the napkin that she had been twisting in her hands. After a moment she looked back at him with renewed composure. "I know now that you didn't want any more children."

She waited a fraction for him to interrupt her before continuing. "It would have been nice of you to have let me know before all that . . ."

"Greta—"

"Did you ever even want Charlotte?" she asked.

It wasn't the first time over the course of the year that she had asked him this. It was unclear to Phillip if she had forgotten his answer, or if she was checking for inconsistencies.

"I wanted *you*, Greta. I wanted Charlotte because you did, and now . . ."

"Now?" Greta leaned forward in her chair.

"Now I can't imagine my life without her." He looked into the painful depths of her eyes. "Or without you," he added quietly.

She blinked at him. "So we get rid of them. Give them away to other . . . happy families. Or we give them to research."

"I think if we had made another child, then I would be okay with the adoption option. Or maybe the stem-cell research?" He shuddered. "Research sounds so gruesome."

"You would be okay with either of those options? Really?"

"I said *if*. If we had made another child, then yes. What I *want* is to go back and start over. To have a second child like we always planned to before . . ."

"It's not going to happen." Her voice was flat and dispassionate.

The cell phone that she had placed on the table lit up with a text. She picked up her phone and tapped out a lengthy reply while holding it in her lap. Phillip looked away to avoid watching her. A crowd of people was gathering near the counter, waiting for their drinks. Abruptly, he noticed Marina, the mother of one of Charlotte's school friends. She was wearing faded cargo pants and a T-shirt with a swatch of blue that read PANTONE #292. He hadn't seen her in months, and he felt a flash of embarrassment at the prospect of running into her now, of all times. She leaned on the counter, oblivious to him, lost in the Arts & Leisure section of a borrowed copy of the *New York Times*. Slowly Phillip turned toward the window, hoping to render himself unidentifiable without also alerting Greta, but at precisely that moment, Marina glanced up from the paper and her eyes met his. She squinted at him but didn't move. He waved to her, and Greta turned around to see what had caught Phillip's gaze. Marina hesitated slightly before approaching the table.

"Hi. How are you?" she asked Greta.

Greta smiled at her. Phillip recognized it as her polite smile reserved for strangers. She started to wave and then, noticing Marina's outstretched hand, she reached out and shook her hand instead. "I'm Marina. Oliver's mom. Charlotte's friend?"

"Yes. Charlotte talks about Oliver all the time. I'm Greta. I know we've met but . . . nice to meet you again."

Phillip drank the rest of his coffee and looked desperately into his empty cup, concentrating all of his energy on willing Marina to leave.

"Large Americano for Marina!" the goateed barista called out. "Marina!"

"That's me," Marina said, turning to leave. "Have a good weekend, you two."

"Thank you," Phillip said. As Marina walked away, he exhaled, only then realizing that he had been holding his breath during the women's entire exchange.

Greta watched her retreat and then turned back to Phillip. "I keep forgetting her name."

He nodded.

"Do you know her?"

"Charlotte and her son, Oliver, used to have playdates."

Greta cocked her head slightly. "Used to? What, they don't anymore?"

"Not for a few months," Phillip said. "I thought maybe they went away for the summer."

Greta raised her voice. "So you *do* know her." She turned around to see if Marina was still there.

"Through her son. They played together . . ."

"You like redheads . . . never mind." Greta picked up her cell phone and tossed it into her purse. "Don't tell me. I don't want to know."

The following weekend Greta headed down the 405 South to pick up Charlotte, who was returning on the 7:55 p.m. flight from Seattle, at LAX. Greta sped down the freeway grateful for the steady flow of traffic. She turned the radio to a science show on NPR, trying to distract herself from thinking about Peter, whom she had left minutes earlier at his beach apartment.

He had just received an unexpected offer to play a small but pivotal role in a television movie that was shooting in Canada, and he had asked Greta to come with him. The part was of a janitor at a small women's college who is the first victim to fall prey to a band of sorority werewolves. He was set to fly to Vancouver that Wednesday.

"I thought werewolves were men," Greta said.

"The director has a feminist take on it," Peter told her. "And he has a background in music video," If he was aware of his non sequitur, he didn't acknowledge it. He dropped to the floor and started doing push-ups.

Of course, Greta knew that he was an actor. She herself had watched Peter when Charlotte was in preschool. But in the months they had spent together, either by choice or design, the topic of the children's show that he had been the long-standing host of rarely came up. *Peter & Pooka* had been one of Charlotte's favorites and Greta had even bought the first three seasons of it on DVD, much preferring Peter's voice to that of the whiny and fearful Caillou or the boundlessly enthusiastic Dora who seemed never to stop screaming. "SWIPER, NO SWIPING!" Peter's voice was pleasant and relaxing, and unlike with the other frenetic animated shows, Greta found that she was able to sleep while Charlotte immersed herself in the universe of *Peter & Pooka*. Sleep. An act whose merits are wholly underappreciated except by victims of torture and by new parents.

It took at least a month of knowing the real Peter for Greta to stop inadvertently yawning whenever she heard his voice. She confessed this to him one night as they lay on their backs on sleeping bags in his empty apartment, thinking it would make him laugh. Instead, it had the opposite effect. The amiable humor that had attracted her since she had known him vanished. Helpless and embarrassed, she watched him as his face darkened. Almost immediately he apologized, but she refrained from discussing his acting career after that and was surprised when he sprang the Canadian movie on her.

"It's kind of a big deal to get this offer," he had told her after completing a set of push-ups. "I just signed with APA less than two weeks ago, and to get an offer that quickly is a huge vote of confidence."

Greta nodded as she regarded the flush of excitement in his face. His color was lighter and brighter than she had seen it since she had met him, and she became aware for the first time how important his acting career was to him. For reasons that she wasn't even sure of (fear? convenience?) she had incorrectly assumed that his acting was something that he no longer cared about. He rarely spoke of it except to make the occasional self-deprecating comment about the show, and she'd had neither the thought nor inclination to investigate further.

"I'm really happy for you, Peter." She sat down on a box with BOOKS scrawled across the side. He sat across from her in the middle of his still nearly empty apartment. "But I don't think I'll be able to join you. Maybe for weekends . . ."

Peter frowned. "But you don't have a job."

"I have Charlotte."

"I know you have a kid," he said.

His comment unnerved her. The word was harmless, but the way he said "kid" sounded to her like "dog" or "houseplant." An inconvenience that needed to be fed and watered, looked after by single friends on vacations. Her face must have betrayed her because he smiled and extended his sneakered foot toward her, tapping the toe of her shoe.

"Vancouver is supposed to be incredible for children. . . ."

From outside the window a woman jangling a can of coins called out, "*Hep hep hep the homeless.* . . ." Peter listened for a moment and then walked over to the window and lowered it. He came back and sat next to Greta on the floor. She reached out and ran her hands through his hair. His hair was so different from Phillip's. Longer, coarser, and curlier. She could never get the thought out of her mind that she was touching something that didn't belong to her. Peter closed his eyes and leaned his head on her knee.

"She's starting school in a couple of weeks," Greta finally said.

"Second grade? First grade?"

"First grade."

"So what's she going to miss if she's a couple weeks late? The Pythagorean theorem?"

"No . . ."

"Are they dissecting Gaddis?"

Greta stared at him. A frustration with his utter lack of understanding began to gnaw at her, like wearing a shoe a half size too small.

"She'll miss making friends. Feeling a part of a community."

Peter raised his head as if he were about to say something. Then he seemed to change his mind and laid his head back down on her knee.

"And anyway, until Phillip and I are divorced, neither one of us can take Charlotte out of the state. Let alone the country."

"Well, there we have it." He gently took her hand from his hair and held it in his on her lap. He kissed her hand before releasing it. "I'll miss you," he said.

He stood up and walked into the kitchen. Greta watched him take a beer out of the refrigerator and open it. He tossed the bottlecap in the direction of the makeshift trash and missed.

It was exasperating that he could be so oblivious about what it meant to have children. She already deeply regretted letting her daughter know that she was seeing another man romantically, and she was sure that if she hadn't had such a fragile command over her own emotions, she would have trusted her own better judgment and waited. From the moment he met Charlotte, Peter had valiantly tried his best to charm her, confident that all children were predisposed to like him. Charlotte, however, was a proud outlier. She resolutely refused to accept him. She declined to speak to him, challenged Greta on the most basic request, and as her grand denouement, she began sucking her thumb around Peter, a habit she had quit at two years old. After that, Greta stopped trying to do anything with the two of them together.

Instead of being more sensitive to her plight, it felt to Greta that the less Peter saw of Charlotte, the less she existed for him. She became a tiny, inconvenient abstraction. She wanted to scream at Peter, "But she *is* me! You can't say you are in love with me and not love *her!*" But she also knew that you can't make anyone love someone any more than you can make them *not* love someone.

They did their best to reconcile before she had to leave for the airport, but Peter's persistent sullenness pervaded the apartment just as the moisture from the sea permeated his walls and settled into the cracks and dripped from the ceiling—the same wetness that warped the book covers and caused the upright piano that he had shipped from New York to promptly fall out of tune.

They sat glum and silent on the mattress in the bedroom as Greta helped to organize his duffel bag for Canada. She rolled his mismatched socks into balls and folded the T-shirts, separating the short- and long-sleeved, while Peter thumbed through a graphic novel.

When she emerged from his apartment, she hurried down the rickety wooden steps and ran to face the water, hungrily gulping in the ocean air. By the time she put the key into the ignition of her car, she felt exhausted, crushed by the unpleasant sense that she was doing nothing more than driving from one child to the other.

Greta had just reached the short-term parking lot at LAX when she received a call from the airline informing her that her mother had neglected to sign the release form for Charlotte. Despite being paged several times, Greta's mother was unreachable and the airline would be unable to hold the flight any longer.

"But she's six years old!" Greta cried. "I'm here at the airport waiting for her."

"I understand that, Mrs. Parris," the representative said. "But we have rules which clearly state the guardian at the location must sign the release form for the unaccompanied minor and must also stay until the plane departs."

"I understand," Greta moaned. "Can you just let me try to locate my mom? Or maybe have my father come to get her? He can take a cab. . . ."

Greta was told that Charlotte would be in the care of an employee from the airline, and depending on how long it took to locate Greta's parents, there was a chance Charlotte could take the later flight, scheduled to depart within the hour. Greta frantically dialed her mother, father, and nephew but reached the voice mail for each one. The last person she dialed, and the only person to pick up, was Phillip.

By the time Phillip arrived at the airport Greta had already received the news that Charlotte would have to be sent on the first flight out in the morning. Her mother hadn't realized her error and was surprised to arrive home to find Charlotte seated at the table eating pizza with her husband and grandson. Greta was still yelling at her mother for leaving her cell phone in the car when Phillip took the phone from her and calmly spoke to a rattled and defensive Ilse.

"It's hard to remember things at my age," Ilse cried. "They didn't tell me that I had to sign any form. We didn't used to have to do that!"

Phillip reassured her that everything was fine, and they would pick up Charlotte in the morning. Greta followed his Volvo to the overnight parking lot and then he took over the wheel and drove a shaken Greta back to what had once been their home.

Phillip hadn't been in any room other than the kitchen and Charlotte's bedroom since they had separated, and feeling disconcertingly like a stranger, he followed Greta into their bedroom. She talked to him over her shoulder as she headed into the bathroom to shower.

"Can you open a bottle of something?" Greta called out. "I want some wine. There might be something open on the counter."

He turned and circled back toward the kitchen, marking the small, subtle changes that had taken place since he had left. The walls had been painted a shade or two darker. He peeked into what was formerly his office and found it stacked high with file boxes that didn't belong to him. Upon closer inspection, he noticed the word "Layton" scrawled across the sides.

The sisal rugs that had been on the floor since they moved in were replaced by Turkish kilim rugs. For years they had talked about investing in the expensive rugs together, and now it looked like Greta had taken the initiative. The rugs were warm and imperfect and made the modern, forbidding walls of the showpiece house they had built together seem for the first time like a home.

Charlotte's room was the only room that was unchanged. It was also the only place that contained a picture of Phillip and Greta together. It was of the two of them in Spain. They had asked a passing man to take the picture outside of the Prado. They had unknowingly asked a man who was in town curating an exhibit on Goya. When he found out that they were on their honeymoon, he invited them to attend a private showing following a cocktail reception. In the photograph, Phillip had his arm wrapped around Greta's waist, and they were both laughing. He wished now that he could remember at what. Phillip placed the photo back beside the framed picture of Charlotte and Thinmuffin when she was a kitten.

In the kitchen, Phillip found an open bottle of Sangiovese on the counter next to the stove. He opened the cupboard where the wineglasses were kept and found that they had been inexplicably relocated to another cupboard. He poured two glasses and waited for Greta.

She appeared in the kitchen wearing a white tank top and jeans with a towel wrapped around her head like a turban. Phillip handed the glass to her, and she sat down on one of the stools next to the counter. Greta had always been the most beautiful to him when emerging from water. Swimming pools, oceans, bathtubs. He didn't realize that he was smiling at her until he noticed her expression change.

"What?" She eyed him with suspicion.

He paused, considering whether to tell her what he felt. He had sworn off anything vaguely complimentary for months now, sensing that it only served to hurt her.

"What?!" she insisted.

"You look beautiful," he said.

"Why do you tell me that?" She undid the turban, running it across her short wet hair.

"Because I'm thinking it. I'm sorry. I know you don't want to hear it."

She shrugged. "It isn't unpleasant. I just don't know why you tell me that now. It makes me think you want something." Greta swirled the wine around in her glass. She held it up to the light and then brought it up to her lips for another sip. "My fucking mother. Who doesn't keep a cell phone on them when they are watching a child?"

"Your fucking mother," Phillip said, smiling.

Greta shook her head. "It's like she does it on purpose." She took the bottle off of the counter to pour herself some more wine, but it was empty. She walked over to the pantry and took out another bottle. Greta had never been much of a drinker, and Phillip felt slightly wary as he watched her fussing with the corkscrew, the bottle tucked under her arm.

"Let me get that for you." He reached his hand out. "Maybe we should eat something?"

She handed him the bottle and opened the refrigerator. She bent down on her knees and moved jars and old take-out boxes around. "I don't have a lot in here." She took out an egg carton and opened it up, counting the eggs. "I could make omelets. I think I have some onions and hang on—" She opened up the vegetable drawer and located one red pepper, which she held up triumphantly. "Ta-da!"

Phillip refilled their wineglasses and put the cork back in the bottle.

"It sounds perfect," he said. "If it isn't too much trouble."

Greta rolled her eyes at him. "I cooked for you for over twenty years. I think I can manage an omelet now."

She fetched a bowl from under the stove and cracked the eggs into them. She added a splash of milk.

"I hope this doesn't mean that Charlotte isn't going to want to go and visit my parents anymore," she said as she beat the eggs into a yellow froth.

"She sounded fine," Phillip said. "It was probably an adventure for her."

Greta shook her head. "Things can be scary when you're six years old. Last week she wouldn't go to sleep in her own bed for three nights after she found a spider in her room."

"What can I do?" Phillip asked, gesturing to the bowl.

Greta tossed him an onion. "Julienne that," she said.

He took a knife off the magnetic strip on the wall and began peeling the layers away. As he sliced through the middle of the onion, the enzymes released in the air stung his eyes. He pressed on his eyelids with the back of his hand. "You're trying to make me cry."

"Turnabout is fair play," she said.

She replaced the carton of milk in the refrigerator and took a sip of wine. "Thinner," she said, pointing to the onions with the tip of her own knife. She took her place at the counter next to him and started chopping the pepper into skinny red pieces. "Like this," she said. They stood shoulder to shoulder, chopping silently.

"Did I ever tell you about the time that my parents forgot me in a shopping mall?" Phillip asked. He handed her the small plate with the onion and leaned back against the counter. Greta emptied the onion into a sauté pan with the pepper. She switched on the overhead fan.

"What do you mean they forgot you?"

"My mother was there to buy a paper that was running an ad for our restaurant. I guess they couldn't find it at any of the newsstands, so my mom ran in with me to the bookstore and my father stayed out in the car listening to a ball game on the radio. It must have been around the same time of year as now. Dad was obsessed with baseball. He had hoped to play professionally at one point. I didn't know that until after he died."

Phillip paused for a moment, wiping his eyes with the back of his wrist. "So, we went into this bookstore that had a good magazine stand, and while she's looking through the paper, I wander away to check out at the scratch-and-sniff books in the kids' section. Remember those?"

"Loved them." Greta reached behind the stove for some rock salt. She sprinkled a few grains over the vegetables and tossed the remainder over her shoulder.

"I don't even think I was in school yet, so that was about the level I was at. After a while, a grown-up—must have been an employee—comes up and tells me that I'm scratching the books too hard, and if I want to read and scratch, then I'm going to have to buy it. So, I got up to go find my mom and she's gone."

"What do you mean gone?"

"No idea. She just left. And I was too young to know my telephone number, didn't even know my parents' first names. I just knew Mama, Papa, Tony, and my own name."

Greta lowered the heat and stirred. The onions were beginning to change color, becoming translucent.

"Were you scared?"

Phillip was thoughtful for a moment. "No. I mean, maybe in that first rush of finding that I had been left. I suppose I must have been scared. I had to have been, right? I imagine I cried. But honestly what I remember more than that was the attention. I was taken into a room. Given candy—which was a big deal considering that my parents wouldn't even let us have sugarcoated cereal like all the other kids. Tony used to call me the Little Prince, but for once I was actually treated like one."

Greta smiled. "Little Prince. I remember that. It was featured heavily in his wedding toast."

"Jesus." He laughed. "What an epic disaster."

"Foreshadowing," Greta said.

Phillip sighed. "No, Greta. Not foreshadowing. Alcohol."

"Anyway, what happened to you at the bookstore? I'm surprised you never told me anything about it."

"I didn't remember it. Until today. Thinking about Charlie at the airport." He paused, remembering the excitement in Charlotte's voice when she told him about the game that she was playing on the airline employee's iPad.

"I didn't want to go back," Phillip told Greta. "I would have been happy just staying with these big benevolent strangers, drinking soda, eating candy, playing tic-tac-toe. Feeling like someone special. It was like a little whiff of celebrity. Or what I imagine celebrities must feel. What draws them to it."

"How long until you were reunited with your parents?"

"My parents showed up, it was probably only a half hour later. The look on their faces made me feel so ashamed that I had taken any pleasure in the adventure. They looked . . . stricken. I remember how red my mother's eyes were. My father's jaw was locked. He was furious. Clearly blaming my mother for her absentmindedness. She had been terrified. Both of them were."

Greta flipped the soft vegetables in the pan with a wooden spoon.

"We never talked about it. Even years later, my mother was too ashamed to discuss it. And I never allowed myself to get lost again." Greta looked up when she heard Phillip's voice break, but he had turned his face away from her; all that was visible was a fraction of his profile, contorted and grieving. "I'm sorry," he mumbled. "I just miss you. Our family. I know you don't want to hear it. I didn't mean to start."

He wiped roughly at his eyes with the cuff of his shirt, angry with himself for breaking down in front of Greta. He found his weakness humiliating; already she thought of him, he knew, as tedious in his remorse, and the last thing he wanted was to confirm this dingy portrayal of himself. He was surprised, then, when Greta reached out and touched the top of his shoulder. He hadn't been expecting it—he couldn't remember the last time she had deigned to touch him—and in a kind of disbelieving trance, he laid his cheek on her hand. She left it there, and he rubbed his cheek across the back of her hand. After a moment, she gently removed her hand and returned her attention to the eggs. She molded the egg mixture into one hefty omelet, which she transferred onto a single plate.

He met her at the table, and together they ate the omelet. It was warm and salty, and he took large, greedy bites. The intimacy in this simple pleasure, an intimacy that had been absent since they fell apart, left him ravenous, and when the omelet was gone, he desperately wanted to go back and make it again.

Greta got up and put the plate in the sink. The forks clattered as they slid from the porcelain onto the stainless-steel basin. She ran the water for a moment, and he watched her shoulders grow still, in that quiet, certain way of hers. Then she switched off the water and came back to the table. She took both of their glasses and carried them to the bedroom. He followed her.

Greta lay wakeful next to Phillip, who slept beside her. She hadn't intended to go to bed with him, but now that she had, she tried to stop herself from feeling the dull ache of regret. Not to say that she hadn't enjoyed it. The firmness of his broad back, the soft blond patches of hair across his chest and circling his navel, everything about him was both familiar and new. She had urged him on faster, consoling herself with the pretext that if it happened quickly enough, she could put it out of her mind, deny that it had ever occurred. But Phillip restrained her movement, delaying the mutual rush of restive desire. "I don't know if this will ever happen again," he had said. And so they had lingered, abating the urge onward to the inexorable and exquisite little death.

Now she lay on her back thinking of her betrayal. Granted, Phillip was still her husband, and the commitment that she and Peter had made to each other was tenuous at best, but still Greta found it troubling how easy it had been to relinquish the standards that she held up for herself.

What had this changed for her? There was the small comfort of knowing that Phillip was still attracted to her—a fact that she had doubted, even though everyone from the marriage therapists to her friend April (whose own marriage had ended in a bonfire of infidelity years before) to Phillip himself had avowed. Still, the doubt had always persisted, the result of what she considered her linear mathematical thinking. Mathematics had always come easy to her because it embodied absolute justice—everything was reconcilable as long as you did the same to either side of the equals sign. Every question had a simple, direct, discoverable answer. Each puzzle could be pieced together, every mystery solved. Now only the questions remained. The answers simply didn't exist, not in any way that would ever satisfy her.

Still, there were some questions that for practical purposes had to be answered. Six frozen embryos. Six potential children. The boy that she had hoped for, another possible green-eyed, towheaded baby girl like Charlotte. Six lives to nurture, the wild or docile schoolchildren they would become, the surly teenagers, arrogant young college students, and weary adults with families of their own to raise. Greta knew that it was next to impossible that all of the embryos would be viable—there was no assurance that even one of them would survive after being implanted into her uterus—but as long as they existed, preserved by medical science, those six embryos were suspended in the balance of her and Phillip's vague and volatile union.

For as long as she could remember, Greta had been in favor of a woman's right to choose what happens to her own body, and there was no question for her that had three embryos implanted in her uterus, she and Phillip would have made the choice to reduce to one. So why did it seem intolerable now to let even one go? Phillip had said that he would agree to release them into the world for other families to adopt, and while this seemed the most practical and generous solution, Greta knew that if she consented, it would eventually drive her mad. She supposed that the arcane biological imperative that supposedly exists for men to spread their DNA far and wide could arguably exist for women and their need to nurture. How else to explain why it was unbearable to Greta that a child, one that shared the same genetic makeup of their own Charlotte, could be out in the world dependent upon the capricious kindness of people entirely unknown. She knew that until the day she died, she would never stop looking for the face of her child in the eyes of strangers.

Phillip stirred next to her. He reached out, waking briefly, but as soon as his hand found the warmth of her body, he settled back into sleep. Greta shifted onto her side and studied his face in the shadowy light. They had found each other when they were still teenagers, and he had always appeared the same to her. Now as she examined Phillip in his sleep, she could see the years in stark relief on his face. She took her finger and ran it across the deep lines etched in his forehead. He opened his eyes and squinted up at her.

"Hey," he said. "Are you okay?" He yawned, covering his mouth with his elbow.

"Those boxes in the office aren't Peter's," she said.

He opened his eyes wider. "Oh, okay. I wasn't going to say anything. . . ."

"They're his sister's. Lindsay. I offered to help figure out her finances. I might work with her, depending on whether I can sort it out."

"That sounds like it could be . . ." He paused. "But what about—are you going to stay with him?"

Greta sighed and fell back onto the bed. "I don't know. I . . ."

Phillip grabbed a pillow. He propped himself up with it, waiting for her.

"No. I don't think so," she said finally. "I don't want to talk about it."

"Okay," Phillip said. They were both quiet for a moment. "Would it be all right if I told you how happy that makes me?"

Greta sat up and turned on the light. He raised his hand to shield his eyes from the glare.

"I don't want to hear about how happy that makes you!" she cried. "I don't want you to be happy."

"Ever?"

"Not in this lifetime."

She began to cry, hating the rage in her, the way it would not leave her, like a sliver embedded deep beneath the flesh, jagged and inflammatory, impossible to extract. Phillip pulled her close to him. She pressed her face against his chest, squeezing her eyes shut. "I'm sorry, Greta. God, if I could change it, you know I would. You *know* I would."

A dog barked, followed seconds later by a siren. They both lifted their heads to see how close it was. As the sound receded into the distance, they turned their attention painfully back to each other.

"Don't you?" Phillip tilted her face up toward his. She shrugged imperceptibly and buried her face back into his chest.

"I love you so much," he said, kissing the top of her head.

"But I'm the same person," she murmured. "There's nothing about me that's different. I'm not any different." She reached over and switched off the light. "Except a year older." She lay on the pillow and stared up at the faint light edging through the blinds.

"*I'm* different," Phillip said in a whisper.

"I would feel weak going back to you." It was the first time that she had said it out loud, the possibility that she might give their marriage another chance. Even in therapy, despite Phillip's entreaties, Greta had never once even hinted at considering a reunion. It had been bad enough to endure the judgment, all those years ago, when she had chosen a man over her own education and career. *These are rights that we won for you*, older women had insinuated. Her mother could barely contain her disappointment. As her former classmates attended graduate school and established careers, then married and started families (where the parenting duties were unabashedly relegated to foreigners), they seemed to Greta to be almost embarrassed by her decision to become a homemaker.

At the time she had felt her choice to stand behind her husband's career achievements while she built a home and family was noble, even as it was judged by others as foolishly old-fashioned. Now she just felt foolish, and the thought of going back to this man after all the pain she had endured suddenly seemed ludicrous.

"You're not weak," Phillip said. "I was the one who was weak. Anyone can see that."

Greta swallowed, not answering. Phillip lay still next to her, for once not trying to pull her into him.

"I don't expect you to try again," he said, "Obviously, I hope—well, you know what I hope. But I'd understand if it was something that you couldn't do."

"Could *you* do it?" Greta asked. "If things were reversed, if I had been the one who . . ." She trailed off.

"I don't know," Phillip said. "I'd like to think, eventually, I would—"

"It would bring you to your knees," Greta said. "To your *knees*."

Phillip exhaled. "What can I do? Or say? Or not do or not

say to make you believe in me, Greta? I'm not where I was. I'll never be in that place again."

Greta ran her hand along the side of his face. Phillip put his hand on top of hers. "Why do you love me?" she said. The question surprised her as much as it seemed to surprise him.

"What do you mean?"

"It's a simple question."

"Well, I mean . . ." In the darkness she could just make out his bewildered profile. She observed the muscles around his eyes tighten as he gauged her reaction. She wasn't certain what she was looking for, but then she saw it: a softening of his expression as he relinquished anticipation, persuasion, his harried and relentless solicitations. A tired, almost serene look came over him. "If you had asked me that a year ago, I would have fallen all over myself trying to answer you. But no matter how much I went on about your beauty or your intellect or your kindness or the times we had together, our shared lives as parents, the truth is . . . that's just part of it. That's just the outside. The inside is the thing that I don't know." He smiled, exhaling deeply. "And it's why I can't stop loving you. There's something about you, and about me, that comes together in a way that doesn't come together when I'm with anyone else. And I hate to think that I spoiled it. That for the rest of our lives, we won't have access to that anymore." Shaking his head, Phillip pressed the back of his neck into the crumpling pillow. "I pray that someday we can make each other happy. I don't know if I can make you happy anymore, Greta, but if there's even the slightest chance of it, I'll wait for as long as it takes."

She wasn't sure when or how it happened, but eventually she fell into a thick and dreamless sleep. She was awakened in the morning by the familiar sound of Thinmuffin mewling and scratching at the door. As Phillip got out of bed to let the cat in, Greta answered the phone on the bedside table. It was her mother calling from the airport in Seattle, informing her that Charlotte was safely on her way back to them.

They left the house in plenty of time to allow for traffic or any other unforeseen mishap on the way, but getting the certificates to pick up their daughter at the gate, and hustling their way through security, took much longer than expected. They appealed to strangers in order to get through the line faster. "*Six-year-old daughter, traveling alone . . .*" They recited their way up the line of weary travelers waiting impatient and shoeless for their turn to put their bags through the X-ray machine. Most were pleasantly, some resentfully, obliging.

Upon being released from security, they ran across the entire terminal to Gate 17 to find that the gate had been changed to 2, which was all the way over by security. They circled back and arrived at the assigned gate, distraught and short of breath, only to be told that the flight would be delayed another ten minutes. Drained, they collapsed into the chairs overlooking the tarmac.

Greta leaned back and closed her eyes. "Charlotte isn't leaving home again until she's eighteen," she said.

Phillip left in search of coffee, while Greta remained near the gate, scanning the sky for Charlotte's plane. Her phone vibrated in her bag. Greta took it out and saw a text from Peter.

I'M SORRY.

She turned off the phone and put it back in her bag. Then she thought better of it and turned it back on.

Over the course of the year she had often wondered if it would feel worse to betray rather than be betrayed. She remembered April, who had deliberately sought out a married man the weekend that her husband had moved in with his mistress. Greta and Phillip had been happy then, and the thought of her friend choosing a married man had been a great source of contention between the two of them. It went against every moral fiber in Greta. Unsuccessfully, she had tried to contain her judgment until April—her best friend dating back to preschool—confronted her one night, drunk and belligerent. She accused Greta of being a "sanctimonious, self-righteous reactionary."

"You can't understand. You still *have* a husband," April had said.

"But he isn't yours," Greta had argued. "It's like you're taking something that doesn't belong to you. He isn't your husband. It's stealing."

"I know he isn't my husband," April had cried. "But he is *somebody's* husband and he wanted *me*."

Now Greta cringed as she considered the intractability of her younger self, her inability to sympathize with anyone else's fragility. Regarding her own betrayal, she felt a discomfort that she supposed to be the weight of her guilt, but that was all. It was nothing like what it had felt like to be the one deceived. There had been times that Phillip had ventured to persuade Greta of the terrible weight of his suffering. He had told her that he would switch places with her if he could. Perhaps it was true. It was a matter of love, she supposed. The quality of betrayal is commensurate only to the measure of love for the one you betray.

Phillip arrived just as the plane was pulling into the gate. He handed her a large coffee. "Sorry, their cappuccino machine was broken." He sat down, bracing the cup between his knees, and tore open a sugar packet to pour into his coffee.

Greta took one of the unopened packets of sugar and put it in her purse. Then she slung her bag back onto her shoulder and stood up.

"I want another year to decide," she said. He looked at her. "I'm not ready to let go of them yet."

Phillip stood up beside her. He reached out to embrace her, and suddenly stopped, uncertain. It was Greta, then, who went to him.

From behind, Greta heard the clarion call of Charlotte. They broke apart and turned to see Charlotte holding the hand of an older female flight attendant. Charlotte dropped the woman's hand and burst into a sprint toward them. As she approached her parents, Charlotte froze, as if suddenly unsure whose arms she should run into.

"Come here, you!" Phillip cried out, scooping her up. Charlotte squealed with delight and reached an arm out to Greta while she wrapped the other one around her father's head.

"Mama."

"She is a lovely young lady," the flight attendant said as Greta signed the airline's release form. "Mine is twenty-seven now," she continued. "I don't know where the time goes."

Greta pulled off the Pacific Coast Highway and onto Ocean Avenue on their way back to the house.

"I painted rocks with Oma!" Charlotte said.

"Is that why your suitcase was so heavy?" Phillip asked. "Because, you know, I was going to ask you if you had rocks in there!"

Charlotte giggled. "Milo helped me find them in the bay. He was painting with me, too, until his ugly girlfriend came."

"Don't call her ugly," Greta said. "That isn't nice."

"But she is!" Charlotte insisted. "And all they do is kiss, kiss, kiss all the time. It's *nauseating*."

Phillip looked at Charlotte and then to Greta. "Where's she getting these words?"

"What?!" Charlotte leaned back and put her feet up on the seat. "Oma says that."

"Mom." Greta shook her head. She slowed down as a jogger jaywalked in front of her.

"Put your feet down, honey." Phillip reached back and tapped on Charlotte's ankles. She dropped her feet, pouting, and then something caught her eye outside the window.

"Oooh! The pier! Can we go? Please, please?"

She leaned forward, sticking her head between the two front seats, arranging her face in the most persuasive expression she could manage. Greta called it her "sick puppy" face. "*Puhlease?*"

Greta looked to Phillip.

"Your call," he said.

The park was mostly empty, having just opened. After they'd purchased the all-day wristband for her, Charlotte ran ahead to choose her first ride. She hesitated between Inkie's Pirate Ship and the Moon Jumper and then chose the latter after finding out that she didn't meet Inkie's height requirement.

"Are you sure you don't want us to go with you?" Phillip asked as Charlotte extended her skinny arm to show the orange wristband to the man at the ride's entrance.

"I'm sure," Charlotte said. "I'm not afraid."

She sat in the center of the empty car with a solemn expression as the man strapped her in and tugged on the belt for safety. He took his time walking back to the controls. Charlotte gave a little wave to her parents and looked up above her head in expectation.

Greta and Phillip stood on the ground together. The man pulled the lever, and all at once they watched their daughter take to the sky.

ACKNOWLEDGMENTS

I would like to thank the following people:

Carrie Kania for not batting an eye when I told her that my second book would be a collection of short stories and for leaving me in very capable hands.

My publisher Calvert Morgan and the whole It! team for their continued dedication and support.

Especially Denise Oswald for her patience and astute editorial eye.

The following people whose love and wisdom have helped immeasurably to support and guide me through the writing process:

Matthew Freeman, Greg Henderson, Brandi Sanger, Meredith Arthur, Julian Fleisher, Julia Caston, James Sanders, Ingrid Bernstein, Molly Ryan, Will Ryman, Alex Auder, Cindy Sherman, Fergus Greer, Todd Thomas, Thomas Weems, Naomi Burns, Venia Skliamis, Hill Salomon, Barbara Foley, Wendy Waddell, Jason Weinberg, Greg Clark, and Victoria Leacock Hoffman.

In particular my friend Darcy Cosper, whose generous assistance and grammatical know-how were invaluable.

Eileen Funke and the Writers Junction.

Ms. Joan Didion for uttering the truest of words: "You must pick the places you don't walk away from." You are the finest inspiration any writer could have.

My fierce and tireless advocate Kimberly Burns. You are worth a thousand and one Burberry trenches.

My agent Susan Raihofer, who somehow makes me believe that I can write anything.

David Daley, who has been patiently waiting for this book for at least a decade.

I would also like to thank my family:

Beth Ringwald Carnes and Dr. Kenneth Carnes, Kelly and Eileen Ringwald, and Chance Podrasky.

Katerina and Makis Tatsos, Irini Gianopoulos, and the memory of Stylianos Gianopoulos.

My parents, Robert and Adele Ringwald, for always trusting my voice.

My children, Mathilda, Adele, and Roman Ringwald Gianopoulos. Thank you for somehow understanding intuitively at such a young age that writing is indeed work and for being such a joy to come home to.

Most of all, I thank my beautiful husband, Panio Gianopoulos. You are my first editor, biggest champion, kindest critic, and greatest source of strength. Thank you for helping me get un-stuck, for believing in my writing, and for always delivering me home from doubt. You are my inspiration, my MFA program, my superhero, my love. Σ 'αγαπώ πολύ.

Molly Ringwald's work in film is characterized by what the renowned *New Yorker* film critic Pauline Kael called her 'charismatic normality'. Throughout her extensive career, she has worked with such directors as Paul Mazursky, John Hughes, Cindy Sherman, and Jean-Luc Godard. Her writing has appeared in the *New York Times*, *Parade*, *Esquire*, and the *Hartford Courant*. She lives with her husband and three children in Los Angeles.

Find out more at
www.iammollyringwald.com
or follow her on twitter @mollyringwald